It would be amusing to teach this man a lesson

"Perhaps I will have that drink after all," Star said.

As she took the brimming glass from him, a few drops fell onto her skin. Laughing provocatively, she made to lick them off, and then, looking straight into his eyes, offered him her wrist instead and whispered suggestively, "You do it...."

To her chagrin, instead of taking up her sensual invitation, he produced a large white handkerchief and carefully dried her skin, telling her quietly, "I'm afraid it's going to stay slightly sticky. Did any spill on your dress?"

"No, my dress is fine," Star told him angrily, snatching her wrist away from him, her skin burning slightly with an emotion that she realized with shock was humiliation.

No man...*no* man had ever reacted to her like that...rejected her like that, and this one was certainly not going to be allowed to be the first.

Dear Reader,

What is more natural than a bride wanting her closest friends also to find happiness in love? For Sally, this means tricking three of her wedding guests into catching her bouquet! Three women, each very different, but each with their own reasons for never wanting to marry. That is why they agree to a pact to stay single, but just how long will it take for the bouquet to begin its magic?

Penny Jordan has worked *her* magic on these three linked stories. One of Harlequin's most successful and popular authors, she has written three compelling romances—all complete stories in themselves—which follow the lives and loves of Claire, Poppy and Star. *Too Wise to Wed?* is Star's story. She's too cynical about marriage to want to marry, but a little bit of seduction would not go amiss!

THE BRIDE'S BOUQUET—three women make a pact to stay single, but one by one they fall, seduced by the power of love

Already available in Harlequin Presents

1883—WOMAN TO WED?
1889—BEST MAN TO WED?

PENNY JORDAN

Too Wise to Wed?

Harlequin Books

TORONTO • NEW YORK • LONDON
AMSTERDAM • PARIS • SYDNEY • HAMBURG
STOCKHOLM • ATHENS • TOKYO • MILAN
MADRID • WARSAW • BUDAPEST • AUCKLAND

ISBN 0-373-11895-3

TOO WISE TO WED?

First North American Publication 1997.

Copyright © 1996 by Penny Jordan.

This edition published by arrangement with Harlequin Books S.A.

Printed in U.S.A.

PROLOGUE

ANOTHER wedding celebration. Star scowled as she studied the elegant invitation before throwing it onto her desk.

She was very tempted to make some excuse not to go—but if she did her friend Sally was bound to pounce on her absence as a sure indication that she, Star, was afraid that the old-fashioned superstition that Sally had practised on the occasion of her own wedding might have some potency to it after all.

Which was all nonsense of course. Just because the other two women who had caught Sally's bridal bouquet along with her had within six months of Sally's own wedding become brides themselves, it did not mean that she, Star, was going to fall into the same trap. No way. Not ever.

She scowled again, even more horribly this time. The fact that Poppy, the other bridesmaid at Sally's wedding, had got married had not come as all that much of a surprise to Star, but the announcement that Sally's stepmother had also married—just a small, private wedding—and was now holding a celebration party with her new husband for all his friends and relations in America... Uneasily, Star stared out of her study window. It so happened that business was taking her across to the States so she could, in fact, make it to the party, and if she didn't go...

If she didn't go Sally would tease her unmercifully about being afraid that there was something in that stupid, old-fashioned tradition that whoever caught the bride's bouquet would be the next to marry.

But weddings were not her thing at all—she had only gone to Sally's because Sally was her oldest and closest friend. After all, she had attended far too many of her father's to have any faith any longer in the durability of the supposedly lifelong vows that people exchanged in the heat of their emotional and physical desire for one another, their compelling need to believe that those feelings would last for ever.

No, weddings, or parties to celebrate them, were quite definitely *not* her scene, and marriage even less so.

But, that being the case, what *had* she to fear in going to Claire's party? Wasn't she, her will, her determination, stronger than any foolish superstition? Of course she was, and, just to prove it, throwing open her window, Star took a deep breath and said firmly and loudly, 'I am not going to fall in love. I am not going to get married. Not now. Not ever. So there.

'Now,' she muttered as she closed the window, ignoring the startled and slightly nervous glance of the elderly lady walking across the lawn in front of the apartment block, 'do your worst, because, I promise you, it won't make any difference to me and it certainly won't change *my* mind. Nothing could. Nothing and *no one.*'

CHAPTER ONE

STAR surveyed the crowd of happy well-wishers surrounding the recently married couple with cynical contempt.

How many of those exclaiming enthusiastically about the happiness that lay ahead of Claire and Brad now that they were married could truthfully put their hands on their hearts and swear that their marriages, their permanent relationships, had truly enriched their lives, had truly made them happy?

If they'd known what she was thinking they would no doubt have questioned the ability of someone who had never been married and who was so vehemently and vocally opposed to any kind of emotional commitment to pronounce on the state of marriage at all, much less to criticise it, but Star believed that she had access to far more experience of what marriage actually was than most of them would be able to boast.

'Star. Claire said you were going to be here.'

Silently Star suffered the enthusiastic hug of her oldest friend.

Sally's voice voice muffled slightly by the thick, smooth, shiny sweep of Star's dark red hair as she continued to hug her whilst telling her, 'I'm so pleased about Ma and Brad, I just wish she wasn't going to be living so far away. It was a wonderful idea of Brad's family, wasn't it, to organise this post-wedding get-together and to invite us all over to share it?

'Has Brad confirmed officially yet that you're getting

the PR contract for the British distribution side of things?' Sally asked as she released her.

'Not yet,' Star told her calmly.

'But you are going to get the contract,' Sally insisted.

'It looks likely,' Star agreed sedately.

'There's only you left now,' Sally teased her friend, changing tack. 'Out of the three of you who caught my bouquet, two are now married, despite the vow that all of you made to stay single.'

Star gave a small, dismissive shrug.

'It was inevitable that Poppy would marry James once she had got over her adolescent crush on Chris, and as for your stepmother...' Star looked thoughtfully towards Claire, who was standing arm in arm with her new husband, her head inclined towards him as they exchanged a small, intimate smile.

'You can stop looking at me like that,' she warned Sally firmly. 'I'm afraid *I* fully intend to be the exception to the rule, Sally. I intend to stay very firmly single and free of any kind of long-term emotional commitment.'

'What if you fall in love?' Sally probed spiritedly.

Star gave her a contemptuously bitter look.

'Fall in love? You mean like my mother, who has fallen in love so many times that even she must have lost count, and who uses that state as an excuse for submerging herself and everyone close to her in a swamp of emotional chaos? Or were you meaning that I should, perhaps, follow my *father's* example and show my ''love'' by begetting children whose existence becomes virtually forgotten when he moves on to a new love and a new commitment?'

'Oh, Star,' Sally protested remorsefully, reaching out to touch her friend's slim, tanned wrist in a gesture of female sympathy. 'I'm sorry. I—'

'Don't be,' Star interrupted her crisply. 'I'm not. In fact I'm grateful to both my parents for showing me reality rather than allowing me to believe in a false ideology. All right, so *my* parents might have taken to un-conventional lengths the modern view that we each have a right to pursue our emotional happiness, no matter what the cost, but tell me honestly, Sally, how many couples *you* can name who remain genuinely happy in their relationships once the initial gloss has worn off.'

'You're such a cynic,' Sally complained on a sigh.

'No,' Star punched back. 'I'm a realist. I accept what, at heart, most women know but cannot allow themselves to accept—that the male human being is genetically pro-grammed to spread his seed, his genes, just as far as he physically can, to impregnate as many women as he pos-sibly can, and *that* is why he finds it biologically im-possible to remain faithful to one woman.

'And that is also why, in my opinion, if a woman wants to be happy she has to adopt his way of life, to enjoy herself sexually when it suits her and not him, to choose her sexual partners because they please her and to refrain from becoming emotionally involved with them, and to remember, if and when she chooses to have a child, that the chances are that she will be the sole emotional support to that child—!'

'Oh, Star, that's not fair,' Sally interrupted her sadly, wincing when she saw the sardonic eyebrow that Star raised in silent mockery to her protest. 'All right, I know that there *are* men like your... Men who do... Men who can't be faithful to one woman,' Sally agreed. 'But not *all* men are like that.'

'Aren't they? But then you would say that, wouldn't you?' Star asked her grimly. 'After all, you've got a vested interest in believing it, haven't you?' she added. 'Speaking of which, how are things between you and Chris at the moment?'

'They're fine,' Sally told her quickly.

Star knew her so well. Too well at times. Star knew how to get under her skin and pinpoint those small, tell-tale areas of vulnerability. She always had done and it didn't even help Sally to remind herself that Star's mode of defending herself and her own vulnerability was to go on the attack. Sally knew how much Star hated any reminders, any discussions about her emotional history, and how prone she was to fending them off by targeting her 'attackers' own weak points.

Not that her relationship with Chris was weak or under threat in any way, Sally hastily assured herself. It was true that just lately Chris had been working longer hours and away from home rather a lot, but...

Sally, suddenly realising that Star had switched her attention to someone else, turned round to see what had distracted her and was rather puzzled when she could see nothing out of the ordinary.

'I must go,' she told Star. 'Chris will be wondering where I am.'

'Mmm...' Star agreed, steadily returning the appreciative interest of a man standing several yards away.

He had been watching her virtually all afternoon, despite his outward absorption in the woman clinging determinedly to his side.

She had two children with her, both of them petite and fair-haired like her. She was quite obviously their mother. Was he their father? Star gave a small shrug. What concern was that of hers?

She was not the kind of woman who deliberately made a play for another woman's man, enjoying the challenge of taking from and competing with her own sex, but neither did she necessarily believe that it was up to her to be the guardian of someone else's relationship.

As a young adult in her late teens and early twenties, she had gone through a phase of sexual experimentation with a variety of short-lived partners. But these days she was extremely choosy—too picky, in fact, or so she had been told—and she was very strict about adhering to a certain set of rules and standards that she had evolved for herself—not, perhaps, the same rules that society hypocritically pretended to live by, but she stuck to hers and they were important to her.

For a start, her partner had to have a clean bill of health and a willingness to prove it. And he certainly had to understand that all she intended to share with him was her sexual self.

She had no inhibitions or hang-ups about the physical side of her nature. Why should she have? If nature hadn't intended a woman to enjoy sexual pleasure then she wouldn't have equipped her with the means to do so, and, that being the case, it was more of a sin, in Star's book, to deny herself that sexual pleasure than to enforce on herself a set of antiquated rules which had been imposed on women by men to preserve their own self-bestowed right to enjoy their sexuality whilst denying women the right to enjoy theirs.

Last but not least, her partner had to accept with good grace the fact that once the sexual excitement of their relationship had faded it was time for them both to move on, although not necessarily, in her case, to another lover.

These days she spent more time in bed alone than with someone else, and, if she was honest with herself, she had grown to prefer it that way.

When her father had walked out on her mother and she had witnessed the financial and emotional devastation that his absence had caused, despite her youth, she had made herself a vow that the same thing would never happen to her, that she would never allow herself to depend financially, or indeed in any way, on anyone other than herself, and that, unlike her mother, she would not keep on falling in love and remarrying in the forlorn hope of finding someone to fill the empty space in her life…in herself…

There were no empty spaces in her life or in her, Star had decided triumphantly three months ago when the arrival of her twenty-fifth birthday had prompted a mental stocktaking of her life.

'Mom, I need the bathroom...'

Star frowned as her attention was abruptly refocused on the small family group that she had noticed earlier by the shrill, insistent voice of one of the children.

The man with them—their father, she assumed—was, she observed, more interested in catching her eye than acknowledging his wife's attempt to capture his attention.

'Clay, Ginny wants the bathroom,' Star heard her telling him.

'Then take her,' he responded impatiently, shaking his head when the woman tried to insist that he went with them.

The look he gave Star as his wife gave in and walked away from him with their children across the lawn of Brad's large family home—built on the shores of the lake around which lay the small American town where he and his family lived and to which he had brought his bride, Sally's stepmother—was one she had seen in very many pairs of male eyes before his.

Barely waiting until his wife and children were out of sight, he started to make his way towards Star.

Star did nothing. She simply stood still, watching and waiting.

He *was* quite attractive, she decided judiciously, though not so attractive as he obviously believed, but then she quite enjoyed a certain amount of confidence in a man, as well as that very obvious streak of selfishness, provided he did not bring it to bed with him.

A selfish lover was not to her taste at all.

As he came towards her she did not, as another woman might have done, exhibit any self-consciousness. There was no need for her to raise flirtatious fingers to the silky dark red satin of her hair which today she was wearing loose over her shoulders in a smooth, polished, immaculate fall. Nor did she need to check any other details of her appearance or draw attention to her sensuality.

The simple silk and linen dress that she was wearing had been bought in Milan and it showed. It fitted the slender, elegant line of her body perfectly. That was to say, it merely hinted at the feminine curves that lay beneath it rather than hugging or emphasising them in the way that the dress worn by the woman who had been clinging so desperately and so unsuccessfully to the man's side had done.

Star never wore clothes which drew attention to her sexuality—there had never been any need for her to do so—not even in bed, where the only thing she wanted next to her own skin was that of her lover.

Behind her she could still hear the querulous voice of the child and the equally irritated response of her mother.

Star's make-up, like her hair and her perfume, was understated. Her father might not have given her his physical support or indeed his financial support during her childhood, but he had given her his excellent bone structure, and by his absence he had also given her the opportunity to witness, at first hand, the folly of trying too hard to please his sex.

Not that she would ever have been tempted to try to appeal to this particular specimen of it, she decided, abruptly changing her mind about her admirer's potential as she observed the smug satisfaction in his eyes—and the lack of humour or intelligence. She might not want to form any kind of permanent or emotional bond with a lover but she enjoyed the spine-tingling ritual of foreplay as much as any other woman, especially when it was spiced with intelligent conversation and laughter.

As she broke eye contact with him with a coolly dismissive look that told him he was wasting his time, she realised that she could still hear the whiny voice of the child behind her and her mother's reproach as she demanded, 'Oh, Ginny, why did you say you wanted the bathroom if you don't? Your father... Oh...'

Star frowned as the woman's tone of voice changed, all its former irritation and lethargy replaced by an almost breathless note of sexual excitement and warmth as she exclaimed, 'Oh, Kyle! Where did you come from? I didn't see you. Clay is—'

'I know where Clay is. I've seen him,' Star heard a coolly incisive male voice interrupting, and she could tell from the way he drawled the words that he knew exactly what Clay had been doing and, moreover, did not approve.

The voice sounded interesting but the man, Star suspected, who not really her type. He sounded far too disapproving and moralistic.

She was just about to walk away and refill her glass with the rather good champagne cocktail that she had been enjoying when a purposeful quartet comprising the two adults she had just heard talking plus the two children—or, rather, a slightly uncertain trio shepherded by an extremely large and very determined sheepdog in the form of a man who would normally have caused her more than a single heartbeat's recognition of his masculine appeal—crossed her line of vision heading towards the man who had just been trying to attract her attention.

There was really no comparison between the two men, Star decided. Clay now looked sulkily, almost seedily unappealing as he ignored his wife's outstretched hand and frowned impatiently down at his two children, whilst the man who had sounded so determined to remind him of his marital and parental status looked...

He looked like the very best kind of sexy American male, Star admitted to herself.

Tall, lithe in the way he moved, he had a sheen of good health on his thick, well-cut dark brown hair and on his forearms where his flesh was exposed by the short sleeves of his snowy-white T-shirt.

She didn't miss, either, the brief glance he gave her as he restored and reunited the small family group—a look which told her how thoroughly he disapproved of what had been going on.

In a flash, the automatic flare of sexual awareness she had felt was submerged by a much stronger flare of resentful anger as she recognised what he was doing. The fact that she herself had already decided that she wasn't remotely interested in the sexual invitation being handed out to her was forgotten as she rose to the challenge of his interference.

Just what the hell did he think he was doing? Star asked herself wrathfully. She had a deeply rooted resentment of other people trying to make her decisions for her, to control her life for her, especially her sex life, and if he thought for one moment that if she'd really been interested in Clay she would have allowed *him* or that theatrical piece of byplay of his to stop her...

Frowning, she started to turn away, shrugging aside her irritation.

It wasn't like her to let anyone get under her skin so easily, especially a male anyone...and especially a male anyone whom she didn't even know and with whom she had barely exchanged more than one assessing glance.

Her frown deepening at the realization that she'd let herself waste time thinking about a man whom she was hardly likely to see again, Star was startled when the subject of her thoughts suddenly appeared in front of her, blocking her path.

Star focused cool aquamarine eyes on him without smiling.

'We haven't been introduced yet,' he began, smiling at her.

His teeth, Star was surprised to see, did not possess the uniform perfection that she had grown used to seeing in American adults. In fact, one of the front ones had a small but very definite chip in it. His smile was slightly lopsided as well, making him look vaguely boyish—something which might appeal to those members of her sex who enjoyed having someone to mother, Star decided scathingly, but she personally preferred her men to be totally and uncompromisingly adult, thank you very much.

'No, we haven't, have we?' she agreed in answer to his comment, with a pointed and wholly unfriendly baring of her teeth, but as she made to sidestep him he stepped with her, still blocking her path.

Star stepped the other way and again he followed her.

'You're in my way,' she told him sharply.

'Your glass is empty,' he commented, ignoring both her comment and her hauteur. 'Let me get you another drink.'

'Thank you, I can get my own drinks *and* anything else I feel I might need,' Star told him evenly.

To her surprise, instead of being offended, he laughed.

'Ah, you're annoyed with me over Clay,' he said, knowingly shaking his head as he added, 'I'm sorry about that, but you would have been rather disappointed. He isn't—'

'Really? You certainly are a very perceptive man,' Star marvelled sarcastically, 'if one look is all it takes for you to know immediately exactly what another person wants.'

'He's a married man,' he returned quietly, the good humour dying from his eyes. His eyes were a very deep, dense blue, shaded by thick dark blunt lashes which, for some odd reason, Star felt compulsively tempted to reach out and touch to see if they felt as soft as they looked.

'Yes, I rather assumed he was,' Star agreed. 'Which was what attracted me to him in the first place,' she added with blithe disregard for the truth. No one, but *no one* had the right to make her decisions for her and she was determined to make sure that this interfering would-be knight in shining armour was made aware of that fact.

'Married men make by far the best lovers,' she went on in deliberate provocation. 'They're normally so grateful to have a receptive, responsive woman in their bed after being frozen out sexually by their wives that they're only too willing to please, and, of course, once the fun is over you can send them home.'

'Fun? You think of sex as fun—something recreational like baseball?' he questioned sharply.

'Yes,' Star agreed, pleased to have pierced the armour of quiet self-assurance that he seemed to wear so easily and so irritatingly.

'Don't you?' she challenged him mockingly.

'No,' he retorted immediately, 'I don't. So far as I am concerned, sex without emotion, without love, without all the things that bond two people together, is like a flower without perfume, initially appealing but on closer inspection a disappointment.'

'That depends, surely, on your outlook?' Star argued, adding when he looked questioningly at her, 'On whether or not you *want* your flower to be perfumed. Some people *don't*; some people are allergic to perfume.'

Trust her, she was thinking ruefully. Outwardly this man, whoever he was, had all the male attributes that most appealed to her. Pity that he'd had to go and spoil it all by opening his mouth and voicing his opinions. An amusing thought suddenly occurred to her, making her eyes sparkle warningly. He deserved to be punished a little for his interference and his high-handed, moralistic manner and she certainly deserved to have a little fun.

She couldn't remember the last time she had devoted her energy to anything other than her work. Her last relationship had been over for— Oh... She was startled

to realise that it was almost two years since she had told
Jean Paul that their long distance affair was over.

She had been celibate for two years! Amazing... Oh,
yes, it was high time she had some fun.

So he didn't believe in sex without emotion, did he?
Well, she didn't believe him. No doubt he found it a
good line with which to blind other women to the truth,
but she was not like other women. No man *really* wanted
commitment... No man *really* wanted a woman's lifelong love. Oh, he might tell you he did at the start of a
relationship, but sooner or later he would revert to
type—to want the challenge of someone fresh, someone
new. Star had seen it happen so many, many times.

Yes, it would be amusing to teach this man a lesson,
to let him believe that he had deceived her with his in-
sincerity, and even more amusing to bring him to the
point where he was forced to admit just how good sex
could be—for its own sake—and she *would* make him
admit it; Star was determined on that point.

'It's normally my sex who express those particular
views,' she told him, letting her voice soften and become
slightly husky, her eyes sending deliberately sensual
messages to his as she played with her empty glass. Then
she breathed, 'Perhaps I will have that drink after all.'

It never mattered how blatant you were or how insincere, Star reflected grimly as he fell into step beside her,
guiding her through the crowd to a hovering waiter with
a full tray of freshly poured cocktails. Men fell for it
every time, greedily swallowing bait that surely in reality
should have choked them.

There hadn't been a man born yet whose sexual ego
didn't outweigh his brains, she decided as she accepted
the full glass he was handing to her.

As she took the brimming glass from him a few drops
fell onto her skin. Laughing provocatively, she made to
lick them off, and then, looking straight into his eyes,

offered him her wrist instead and whispered suggestively, 'You do it...'

To her chagrin, instead of taking up her sensual invitation, he produced a large white handkerchief and
carefully dried her skin, telling her quietly, 'I'm afraid
it's going to stay slightly sticky. Did any spill on your
dress? It might—'

'No, my dress is fine,' Star told him angrily, snatching
her wrist away from him, her skin burning slightly with
an emotion that she realised with shock was humiliation.

No man...*no* man had ever reacted to her like
that...rejected her like that, and this one was certainly
not going to be allowed to be the first.

Stifling her pride and staying where she was instead
of turning on her heel and storming away from him
proved harder than she had anticipated, but somehow she
managed it.

'Are you a member of Brad's family?' she asked him,
subtly studying the contours of his body as she waited
for him to reply.

Those muscles were certainly solid enough. What did
he do? she wondered. Something that involved being
outdoors a good deal of the time, perhaps.

'No, I'm not. Are *you* related to Claire?'

He sounded more polite than genuinely interested but
Star refused to be put off.

'No. I'm actually a friend of Sally, Claire's stepdaughter,' she explained. 'In fact we've been friends since our
schooldays; but I'm not just here as a friend—I'm here
on business as well. I'm a consultant and Brad's been
asking my advice on how to improve the image of their
British distribution arm...'

A slight exaggeration of the truth but justified in the
circumstances, Star excused herself. She was not normally given to exaggerating her own importance—in any
area of her life. It was not normally necessary and she
recognised that she was being far more forthcoming,

supplying him with far more information about herself
than she would normally have done.

But then this was not just about sex, just about meeting an attractive and very sexy man and wanting to go
to bed with him, it was about proving a point, about
confirming one of life's realities, about making him back
down and admit that he was lying when he pretended to
be so emotionally correct and right on!

Engrossed in her own thoughts, Star missed the sudden, startled flare of recognition that darkened his eyes
as he listened to what she was saying.

'So...you won't be attending the family dinner later
this evening, then,' Star commented, and offered tempt-
ingly, 'Neither shall I.'

In point of fact she *had* been invited but she knew
that Sally and Claire would understand if she didn't go.

'No... No, I shan't,' he was agreeing, his impossibly
dark blue eyes—in a woman Star would have instantly
suspected coloured contact lenses but something told her
that this man would never fall victim to such vanity—
meeting hers and causing her pulse to race a little faster.
Oh, yes, he was quite definitely her type, physically at
least.

'So both of us will be at a loose end,' Star prompted.
She was beginning to wonder if she had imagined the
intelligence she had seen in his eyes earlier, he was so
slow on the uptake.

'Yeah, I guess it looks as though we will...' he agreed
in a slow drawl.

'We could have dinner together,' she persisted, 'at my
hotel; I'm staying at the Lakeside,' she added, mention-
ing the town's most luxurious hotel.

'The Lakeside...' He glanced at his watch—a plain,
no-nonsense affair with a worn leather strap, Star noticed. 'I could meet you in the foyer at eight?'

'Eight will be fine,' Star assured him, wondering what
on earth she was letting herself in for.

She said as much to Sally a few minutes later when her dinner date had excused himself and she had bumped into her and Chris walking across the lawn.

'I hope I don't have to work as hard in bed as I had to do to get him to have dinner with me,' she told her friend feelingly.

Sally laughed, although Star could see that Chris looked slightly uncomfortable. Men didn't like it when a woman was sexually aggressive, it made them feel uneasy...threatened.

'Where is he?' Sally demanded. 'Point him out to me...'

'I can't; he's disappeared,' Star told her as she searched the crowded lawn.

'Perhaps he's got cold feet and decided to make his escape,' Chris suggested.

Star gave him a cool look.

'If he has, there are plenty of others to take his place,' she responded.

She could see Sally biting her lip and giving Chris a warning look as he opened his mouth to say something else, but she waited until Chris had excused himself and left them on their own before telling her friend gently, 'It's all right Sally, you don't have to protect me from Chris. I know he doesn't approve of me.'

'It's not that,' Sally protested. 'It's just...'

'It's just that he doesn't like it when a woman behaves like a man?' Star suggested.

'You deliberately try to give him the wrong impression,' Sally defended her husband. 'You make him think...'

'Make him think what?' Star taunted her. 'I make him think that I like sex...that I like men.'

'But you don't, do you?' Sally countered swiftly, shocking Star into silence. Then seizing the advantage she had gained, she continued, 'You don't really like men at all, Star; you despise them. You think that all

men are like your father,' she added sadly, 'and they
aren't. They—'

'No?' Star fought back. 'Tell me that again in ten
years' time, Sal!'

'Oh, Star,' Sally protested under her breath as she
watched her friend stalk off.

'Where's Star gone?' Chris asked his wife a few
minutes later as he rejoined her. 'Off on another man-
hunt?'

'Oh, Chris, she isn't like that. Not really,' Sally protested. 'She just...she's just so vulnerable, really. She
was hurt so badly when her father left her mother and
rejected her, trying to claim that she wasn't his child,
and then there were so many bad relationships in her
mother's life, so many love affairs that went wrong, that
it just reinforced her belief that men can't be trusted.
She tries to pretend she doesn't care—she even jokes
that she can't remember any more how many step and
half brothers and sisters she has got because there are so
many of them—but deep down inside, I know that she
does care, that she—'

'You're far too soft-hearted,' Chris told her lovingly,
curling his arm around her and swinging her round so
that they were face to face. 'I don't know whether it's
all this fresh air or not, but suddenly I am very, very
hungry.'

'Hungry...?' Sally gave him a startled look. 'Chris,
we've only just eaten that wonderful buffet; you can't
possibly—'

'Who said anything about being hungry for food?'
Chris whispered in her ear. 'It's *you* I'm hungry for...
Mmm...and you taste very, very good as well...'

'Chris!' Sally protested as he started to nibble her ear,
but she was laughing as she tried to push him away.

On the other side of the lawn someone else observed
them. He had been watching too when Star had been

with them, had seen her stalk away from Sally in obvious high dudgeon.

It was funny, but although he had heard quite a lot about her both from Sally and from Claire he still hadn't recognised who Star was until she had made that comment about doing some PR work for Brad, Kyle acknowledged.

Listening to Claire and Sally describing her and her background as they'd explained the events surrounding the throwing of Sally's wedding bouquet and the trio's avowed determination to remain unwed despite having caught it, he had felt mildly sorry for the unknown Star and, if he was honest, a little smugly self-satisfied that he was too well balanced to share her warped outlook on life—and he could have done, given his own family history.

His mother had regularly dumped him on whoever she could find to take charge of him whilst she went off with her latest lover. His father had finally and unwillingly taken him under his own roof whilst making it clear how little he wanted him. But happily the bitterness which could have tainted the whole of his life had never been allowed to take root, had in fact been washed away, flooded out by the outpouring of love he had received from his stepmother's older sister, the woman who had become a surrogate mother to him and whom he still gently mourned.

But now...now he had met Star, had witnessed at first hand the powerful, turbulent, magnetic pull of her sexuality, had felt his body respond to it and to her! And it had responded to her... Was still responding to her, if he was honest.

Intellectually he might be aware of all the pitfalls involved in following through on what was running through his head right now, but physically...

He had seen the look she had given him when he had stopped Clay from making his play for her, and the even more contemptuous one she had sent him when he had informed her of his views on sex without emotion. He suspected he knew exactly why she had been so determined to get him to have dinner with her—and it didn't have anything to do with any desire to get him into bed. He only wished that he could say the same about his own motives in accepting.

Right now the thought of all the ways he would like to pleasure her if he had her spread out on a bed underneath him was driving him wild, with the kind of ache that was rapidly becoming a sharp urgency.

For starters he certainly wanted to see that smooth hairstyle all mussed and soft and those challenging sea-green eyes hazy and dazed with the joy of what they were both experiencing, and he surely wanted to feel those full, firm lips quivering eagerly beneath his, clinging to his, whilst he slowly stroked her silky skin. Oh, yes, he surely wanted that.

He wanted to peel her clothes from her body and share with her that spiralling, giddying, breathtaking climb through the delicately, deliberately erotic foothills of shared foreplay, across the plateau of escalating desire and then on to the heights where they could look down on the rest of the universe and momentarily believe that they were superhuman, immortal; but for that it was necessary to reach out and share yourself mentally and emotionally as well as physically and Star had made it more than plain that that kind of intimacy was not on her agenda.

And he had spoken the truth when he had told her that, to him, sex without emotion was like a flower without perfume, and he felt as sad and compassionately sorry for someone who had been denied the ability to experience that emotion as he did for someone who had been denied the gift of sight.

Of course, there had been occasions when he had been growing up when he had thrown himself wholeheartedly into the experience of exploring his sexuality, but since then there had been only two serious relationships in his life—one with a fellow student whilst he'd been at college, which had ended shortly after their graduation by mutual consent, and another which had been over for several years now and which had ended when he had moved from New York City to set up in business here in this quiet, sturdily American small town.

He remained on friendly terms with both his ex-lovers and was godfather to both their eldest children.

It had been the death of Grace, his 'surrogate' mother, that had prompted the heart-searching which had led to the ending of his New York relationship, bringing about as it had the admission that the emotion which he felt for Andrea had become that of a close friend rather than a lover. She had begun to feel the same way, she had confessed when he had finally brought himself to broach the subject with her.

He had promised himself when he'd left New York that the next time, the next love, would be his last, his for all time and beyond time, and, perhaps because of that, or perhaps simply because he was older and wiser and maybe tired too, he had found himself reluctant to embark on any new relationship, sensing that ultimately it would not fulfil his need to form a lifetime bond with that one special woman who would accept him and love him as he was and for what he was, as he would her.

He knew that many of his friends considered him to be something of an idealist. Well, why not? He wasn't ashamed of his feelings, his needs. Why should he be?

And it was only very, very rarely now that his body reminded him that sometimes physical desire and emotional need did not run comfortably in harness with one another—so rarely, in fact, that he couldn't actually remember the last time. So rarely…that it had been tricky getting himself to admit that his determined restoration of Abbie and her two little girls to her roving husband's

side had had less to do with supporting her than with
satisfying his own need to see if the luscious, long-
legged redhead whom Clay was making such determined
eye contact with looked as good from the front as she
did from the back.

She had...unfortunately for him.

He glanced at his watch. It was time he left. He had
some paperwork he wanted to get through. He had just
about made his way to his car when Brad suddenly ma-
terialised at his side.

'Kyle!' he exclaimed, smiling at him. 'Did you get to
meet Star? I meant to introduce you to one another since
you'll be working closely together once you take over
from Tim Burbridge in Britain... I still haven't formal-
ised the details of her contract with her yet, but from
what I've seen of her work there's no doubt in my mind
that she'll do a good job for us.

'Tim Burbridge is taking a month's leave from the
end of next week, as you know, and I'd like the two of
you to meet beforehand so that he can hand over things
to you; of course, you'll be staying on to work alongside
him once he's back at work... I think you'll find him
very co-operative and open. He understands how important it is for us to bring our British distribution network
up to the same high standards we have over here in the
States...

'It won't be easy, though,' Brad warned him. 'One of
our biggest problems is recruiting the right calibre of
technician. Not so much on the technical side—they all
have the necessary skills for the job; no, the problem is
more on the motivation side of things, from what I can
see...'

'Mmm...I've been thinking about that,' Kyle responded. 'I think some kind of in-house training scheme
coupled with incentive awards might be one way around
the problem... But, of course, first I'll have to discuss
things with Tim,' he added diplomatically.

'Well, that's something you and Tim and Star can work on together,' Brad told him. '*Did* you get to meet her?'

'Not exactly... Not officially.' Kyle was deliberately vague.

'Well, I'll make sure that the two of you do get a chance to get together before you fly out to Britain,' Brad promised him.

'You know how much I appreciate what you're doing for us, don't you, Kyle?' Brad asked his friend. 'So far as I am concerned, the distribution network you've set up for us is one of the prime forces underpinning our success. It doesn't matter how good a product is; if you can't get it to the customer when and where he wants it and install it and keep it in good working order, it doesn't matter a damn how good it is.'

Kyle gave a small shrug. 'It works both ways,' he reminded Brad. 'No matter how good a distribution and servicing network is, it can't operate efficiently without a reliable product.'

'We make a good team,' Brad told him, 'and I can't pretend that I'm not hoping you'll be able to help us turn the British side of our business around and bring it into line with our home market success.

'Will you be joining us for dinner this evening?' Brad asked him as Kyle started to unlock his car.

Here was his chance to get out of his dinner date with Star, Kyle acknowledged, and he would be all kinds of a fool...asking for all kinds of trouble if he passed up on it.

Ten minutes later, driving towards his own lake-shore home, contemplating the brief, negative shake of his head and polite words of excuse with which he had responded to Brad's question, he grimaced to himself.

OK, so he was all kinds of a fool!

CHAPTER TWO

IT TOOK Star an unusually long time to prepare for her dinner date with Kyle. It was not like her to dither over what to wear or to question the effect she was likely to have on her date; she dressed to please herself and not anyone else, and yet, for some reason, she found herself eschewing the loose silky cotton dress she had originally decided to wear in favor of a much more sophisticated and slinky one-shouldered black jersey number that she had added to her packing at the last minute on some odd impulse.

Like today's silk and linen dress, she had bought it in Milan where they knew all about the subtle art of emphasising a woman's sensuality rather than her sexuality.

It was not a dress that a man would immediately and necessarily see as provocative. It skimmed the curves of her body rather than clung to them, but the way it exposed the smooth, warm curve of her shoulder and bared one arm, the way it highlighted the fact that one needed a well-toned body and precious little underwear to show it off made it the kind of outfit that bemused men with its subtly sensual message and automatically had every other woman in the room narrowing her eyes warily.

To complement the dress Star had swept her hair up into a smooth chignon and put on heavy, almost baroque dull gold earrings plus a single, matching dull gold bangle.

She was just about to apply her favourite perfume when something stopped her, and, instead of touching it lavishly to her pulse points, she sprayed a small cloud of it into the air and then walked slowly into it. This way the fragrance would be so elusive and subtle that anyone wanting to know if she was truly wearing it would have to move very close to her—very close indeed.

Smiling with satisfaction, she picked up her bag and headed for the door, pausing for a second before turning back and quickly spraying the bed with the same delicate perfume.

So, he liked his roses to be perfumed, did he…? Well, tonight he certainly wouldn't have any complaints. Still smiling to herself, Star stepped out into the corridor.

Whoever had been responsible for the interior design of the hotel was obviously a fan of the *Gone With the Wind* era and had a very romantic streak, Star decided, because the bank of lifts, instead of being situated in the foyer, was actually located on a balconied mezzanine area above it so that one's entrance into the foyer had to be made via a sweeping, curved staircase.

There were, of course, amenity lifts situated discreetly to one side of the foyer, but there was no harm in taking advantage of the props which had so usefully been loaned to her, Star reflected as she paused at the top of the flight of stairs for a moment, firmly refusing to glance downwards in the direction of the foyer to see if her dinner date was there to observe her, before moving elegantly down the stairs in a very fair imitation of the arrogantly graceful prowl that she had seen top models adopt at prestige fashion shows.

Kyle did see her, his brain grimly reinforcing what it had already told him. She looked, he acknowledged as he studied Star's elegant descent from the shadows of the mezzanine, much as he might have imagined some fabled Greek goddess to have looked—almost slightly inhuman in the perfection of her feminine mystery, her profile sculptured, her gaze remote, her body… Hastily

he forced himself not to think about exactly what that
sleek, fluid stretch of matt fabric was concealing.

He was not surprised to see, when he checked the
foyer, that virtually every other man there was watching
her, mesmerised by the strength of her sensuality and
her own indifference to it.

As she reached the last stair he started to walk towards
her. For a second Star almost didn't recognise him. For
some reason she had expected him to look as he had
done earlier in the day and for a moment the sight of
him wearing not a white T-shirt and jeans but an im-
maculately cut dinner suit threw her.

It made him look taller, broader and somehow more
remote, more inaccessible...more...formidable.

Giving herself a small inward shake, Star dismissed
such unproductive and over-imaginative thoughts. He
was still the same man, whatever he chose to wear, whatever outward image he might try to present; inwardly he
was just like all the rest of his sex and, like them, sooner
or later, no matter how much he might try to deny it, he
would prove himself to be as faithless, as worthless as
the rest.

'Never make the mistakes I've made,' Star's mother
had told her emotionally in the first throes of her grief
and anger after Star's father had left. 'Never trust a man,
Star...any man... They'll only hurt you in the end.'

Star, six years old at the time, had taken her mother's
words to heart and learned from them—unlike her
mother, who had gone on allowing her emotions to rule
her life and then regretting it.

He was only a few feet away from her now—more
than close enough for her to be able to look right up
into those astonishingly dense dark blue eyes.

Gravely he returned her gaze—without allowing his
to slide downwards to her body. Star allowed her eyebrows to rise a little as she mentally awarded him a point
for his subtlety.

'We still haven't introduced ourselves,' he announced as he stepped towards her. 'Kyle...Kyle Henson,' he told her, extending his hand.

'Star...Flower,' she told him wryly, adding with a small, dismissive shrug, 'A small folly of my mother's and not, unfortunately, her only one.'

'I'm sorry, I don't quite follow you,' Kyle said.

'It was a joke.' Star shrugged. 'But obviously not a very good one. I was trying to say that my mother's larger folly was not so much in the choice of my name as in the choice of my father...'

'Ah... You don't get on well with him.'

'Well enough,' Star countered. 'Or at least as well as any of the other half a dozen or so offspring he has fathered...and perhaps rather better than most. You see, I have the distinction of having known him the longest and therefore having had the greatest time in which to grow accustomed to his...foibles...'

'You don't like him,' Kyle suggested.

'No, I don't *like* him,' Star agreed. 'So go on,' she mocked as they walked towards the restaurant bar. 'Tell me how shocked you are by my undaughterly emotions and how devoted you are to your own wonderful parents... They are wonderful, of course,' she added, giving him a thin smile.

A man like him would have wonderful parents: a mother who adored and cosseted him, had brought him up to think he was the most wonderful human being that ever lived. And his father would have been stern and silently proud of the boy-child he had produced, reinforcing with everything he did the growing child's belief in himself and his invincibility, his right to live exactly how he chose.

'No, as a matter of fact they weren't,' Kyle told her evenly, and then, before she could cover her shock, asked her, 'Are you always this open and frank with strangers?'

'No,' Star told him, giving him a deliberately seductive half-smile. What she had been intending to do was to shock him a little bit, needle him slightly, but his quiet denial of her comment about his parents, coupled with his obvious lack of any intention of expanding on what he had said, had caused her to change tack. If she couldn't shock him into taking notice of her, then she would have to seduce him into doing so.

In the bar they both ordered spritzers before sitting down to study the menus they were handed.

Although Star was well aware of the interest she was exciting amongst the other diners, she gave no sign of it, and Kyle, who was watching her, wondered wryly how long it had taken her to grow the outer skin of cool self-confidence that she armoured herself in.

That remark about her parents—her father—had been deliberately provocative and he sensed that he had caught her off guard with his response to her taunting comment about his own family background.

Despite the information about herself that she seemed to hand out so freely, he sensed that she was an extremely private person, deeply protective of her innermost self.

'So,' Kyle invited, putting down his menu and smiling across the table at her, 'tell me more about this interesting-sounding family of yours.'

'Interesting?' Star raised her eyebrows and gave him a wry look. 'My mother is currently in the throes of a traumatic love affair with the son of one of her oldest and closest friends. It's supposed to be a secret but, of course, it isn't. My mother couldn't keep a secret if her life depended on it and she certainly can't seem to see that what she's doing is bound to lead to disaster. She's bound to lose her friend, and as for her toy-boy lover...'

'You don't approve?'

Star looked at him. He had surprised her with his invitation to talk about her family. Normally, in her experience, the subject most men preferred to discuss was themselves. Star wasn't used to being asked such unexpectedly intimate questions. One of her strongest character traits was a refusal to deal in any kind of deceit— a fact which put her at a disadvantage now, she recognised, as she found it impossible not to reply honestly to Kyle's questions.

'It isn't a matter of whether or not I approve,' she told him. 'It's more a matter of knowing what's going to happen, of knowing that someone else is going to have to pick up the pieces of the mayhem that my mother's emotional overload always causes...'

'That someone perhaps being you?' Kyle probed.

This time Star could not answer. The anxiety and sense of guilt she had felt as a child, listening to her mother, watching her go through the turmoil of a series of destructive relationships, was something that even now, as an adult, she found impossible to discuss.

The fear she had experienced then, the sense of being alone with no one to turn to, the panic at knowing that she was her mother's emotional support rather than the other way round still sometimes surfaced to attack her present-day, adult self-assurance, even if nowadays, outwardly at least, she had learned the trick of transmuting it into angry contempt for her mother's way of life.

'Why don't we talk about you?' she suggested softly. 'I'm sure that would be far more...interesting...'

Lifting her glass to her lips, she looked across at him as she took a slow, deliberate sip, letting her lips stay slightly parted whilst she looked at his mouth.

At first she thought that her deliberate sensuality had had no effect on him, and then, to her delight, she saw the small, betraying movement he made, the slight shifting of his body, as though suddenly he wasn't quite at ease with himself.

'There isn't much to tell,' Kyle responded, and Star

smiled to herself as she caught the slightly roughened edge to his voice and knew what had caused it.

No matter what he might be trying to tell her, she suspected that he was far from lacking in sexual experience, and from what she could see of it she could sense that his body had just the kind of sensual appeal she most liked.

Star did not believe in being a passive lover and, whilst not having any specific desire to be dominant or aggressive, she did like to be able to take the initiative to touch and taste the man in bed with her, to reach out and stroke his skin, to discover where and how she could most arouse him, even to tease him a little bit sometimes, testing his self-control. And something told her that Kyle would be very self-controlled.

'My parents split up before I was born. My mother had never wanted a child. Her ambition was to be an actress.'

Star frowned as she heard not condemnation in his voice, as she had expected, but, instead, compassion. He felt compassion for a mother who had rejected him? A tiny feather-brushing of unease—no more—disturbed the deep waters of her conviction that all men were the same, that all men were, in essence, her father—a feeling so vague that it was easy for her to dismiss and ignore it and tell herself that Kyle was even more devious than she had first suspected and adept at manipulating the vulnerability of the female psyche.

'Unfortunately she died before she could realise it,' Kyle continued. 'An undiagnosed heart defect. Before her death, though, there had been…problems…and ultimately my father agreed to take me in and bring me up alongside his second family… I was very lucky…'

'How—in being allowed to grow up alongside them?' Star enquired mockingly.

He couldn't deceive her. She knew all about how it felt to watch the father who didn't want you favouring

some other child whilst you looked on in impotent grief
and rage.

'In a sense, yes,' Kyle told her evenly, ignoring her
sarcasm. 'You see, my stepmother had an older sister
who… Well, let's just say she was a very, very special
person and she kinda took me under her wing…helped
me to understand…to develop a proper sense of myself…taught me what it was like to be loved and val-
ued…and that's something I guess every child, and
every adult too, needs…'

'Here endeth the first lesson,' Star taunted softly under
her breath, but if Kyle had heard her he wasn't responding to her taunt. Instead he was looking at the
menu.

'Would you recommend the sea-bass?' Star queried
with mock-feminine deference.

But Kyle refused to be drawn, commenting only, '*I*
certainly like it.'

'Well, then, I'll just have to try a taste of yours, won't
I?' Star flirted, refusing to give up.

It was only a matter of time, Star told herself confi-
dently. With time and persistence she would be able to
prove to her own satisfaction that underneath the dis-
guise of chivalrous knighthood that he chose to wear he
was just as untrustworthy, as selfish and careless of other
people's feelings as the rest of his sex.

Not that it was going to be all hard work getting him
to back down from his claim that, for him, sex meant
nothing without emotion. Unlike men, she did not need
the crutch of self-deceit for her ego. It wasn't simply to
prove a point that she intended to challenge him—and
to win. She had already acknowledged the heightened
buzz of sexual awareness that being with him was giving
her.

The *maître d'* was hovering, waiting to take their order. Star's mouth curled in a small feline smile as she
chose one of the vegetarian options, her smile deepening

as Kyle ordered the sea-bass. Before handing the menu back to the *maître d'* he murmured something to him that Star couldn't hear.

Several minutes later, as a waiter escorted them to their table, Star was amused to see the way the other diners watched them whilst trying to pretend that they were not doing so.

'We seem to be causing something of a stir,' she murmured dulcetly to Kyle as they sat down. 'I wonder why...?'

'Oh, no, you don't,' Kyle countered evenly, smiling at her. 'You know perfectly well that there isn't a single man in the place who has been able to take his eyes off you since you came down those stairs.'

Kyle wasn't quite sure how he expected her to react to his comment, but the sudden warm peal of totally genuine laughter she gave as she acknowledged the truth of his comment made him realise that she was not as predictable and true to type as he had originally assumed, and that whilst with a little conscious effort he should be able to withstand the sensual heat of her deliberate come-ons to him, resisting the effect of that wholly natural laughter and the rueful intelligence in her eyes was going to be much, much harder.

So it was with relief that he observed her revert to type, and he was thrown as she asked him softly, 'Not a *single* man... Does that include you?'

'I'm as visually attracted to a beautiful, sensually dressed woman as the next man,' Kyle replied drily.

It was not exactly the reaction she had hoped for but it would do—for a start, Star told herself as the waiter brought their starters.

Star had ordered mussels, which she picked up with her fingers and ate with a deliberate, almost greedy relish, triumphantly conscious of the fact that although Kyle affected not to be he was acutely aware, as he ate his way stoically through his seafood platter, of the sensuality in the way she was eating.

When she had had enough she licked the juice from the tips of her fingers with deliberate enjoyment, enthusing, 'Mmm...that was delicious.'

There were several mussels still left on her plate and as she made eye contact with him she picked one up and held it out to him, offering, 'Here, why don't you try one?'

His calm, 'I already have, thank you,' as he indicated the empty shells on his own plate, would have caused a lesser woman to retreat in a self-conscious fluster of embarrassment, Star acknowledged, but she was not so easily discomposed. Why should she be? She knew already that he wanted her. Now it was simply a matter of making him admit it.

As she smiled into the bemused eyes of the young waiter who had come to take their plates, she mentally congratulated herself on her inevitable victory and settled back to enjoy the rest of the game.

Their main courses arrived and were served—her own very appetising vegetarian dish and Kyle's sea-bass.

Star waited until they had been served before recommencing her attack, pouting slightly as she eyed her own plate and then Kyle's.

'The bass *does* look good...' she began.

There was something in the dark blue steadiness of his gaze as he returned her eye contact that wasn't, somehow, quite in line with his predictable, 'Would you like some?'

'I thought you'd never ask,' Star responded softly, already leaning towards him, reaching out with one hand to hold his wrist as he lifted his fork towards her mouth, when out of the corner of her eye she saw him make a small gesture towards the *maître d'* and then saw, to her chagrin, their waiter hurrying towards their table, carrying a small portion of the sea-bass.

She could see Kyle watching her urbanely as the
waiter served her with the fish, all her earlier good humour and sense of triumph evaporating in the smoul-
dering fury of knowing that he had not only anticipated
her move but very skilfully sidestepped it as well.

Star wasn't used to men rejecting her sexual advances;
she wasn't used, in fact, to having to make them. It
wasn't normally necessary and for a moment the sheer
shock of having the tables so neatly and unexpectedly
turned on her held her completely silent.

'So you're a PR consultant,' Kyle commented as he
calmly ate his own fish.

'Yes,' Star agreed coolly. 'I trained with one of the
large London agencies and then decided to set up on my
own...'

'It's a very stressful and competitive business, especially—'

'For a woman?' Star supplied challengingly for him.

'For anyone,' Kyle corrected her. 'Especially when
you're working on your own.'

'I like stress...and competition,' Star told him. Was
he trying to find out if she was involved with someone?
If she had a partner...a backer...another man in her life?
Determinedly she pushed her chagrin at his refusal to
respond to her flirtatious teasing over the fish to one side.
If he was interested in finding out if there was another
man in her life then that was a good sign.

'And I'm certainly far from being the only woman to
set up in business on her own,' she added.

'True,' he agreed. 'They do say that the type of person
most likely to succeed in business on their own is one
who enjoys taking control of their own life.'

'And you don't approve of the female sex wanting to
take control?' Star asked softly, feeling that she was getting back on firmer ground.

'Not at all,' Kyle contradicted her. 'It's just that I
often wonder if it isn't so much a need to take control

of their own lives as a fear of being in a situation where they are not in control that is the real emotion motivating such people—a fear of making contact with others, of being open to them...and vulnerable to them...that drives them into isolating themselves—'

Star stared at him across the table as he broke off to shake his head as the waiter offered him more wine; she was torn between an aggressive desire to deny what he was saying and a passively wary one to ignore it.

'I own and run my own business too,' she heard him saying as the waiter left, 'and...' He started to frown as he realised that she had stopped eating, and asked her solicitously, 'Didn't you like the bass, after all?'

'The bass is fine,' Star told him stonily, 'but the conversation isn't.'

Kyle gave her a thoughtful look.

Those dark blue eyes really were dangerously deceptive, Star acknowledged. The extraordinary depth of their colour tended to make one focus on that, rather than on the intelligence behind them.

Suddenly she felt extraordinarily tired. Delayed jet lag, she told herself. She had a meeting with Brad in the morning, for which she needed to be fresh and alert. The last thing she needed was to spend the evening with some pseudo new man whose idea of foreplay was to psychoanalyse her. But she couldn't retreat now without getting at least some tacit admission from him that he did want sex with her; her pride wouldn't let her.

She thought quickly and then decided what to do.

'I'm sorry,' she apologised faintly, 'but I'm not feeling very well.' She gave him a softly rueful look. 'I wonder if you could help me to my room...?'

'Of course.'

Star could see him frowning as he quickly summoned the waiter.

'Would you like me to arrange a house call from the hotel's doctor?' he asked her concernedly.

Star shook her head.

'No…no…it's nothing, really… Just delayed jet lag mixed with too much sun this afternoon,' she explained. 'Nothing a good night's sleep won't put right…'

He had certainly been very efficient at settling their bill and getting them out of the restaurant with the minimum fuss and delay, Star had to acknowledge a few minutes later as they waited for the lift.

Once it arrived and the doors opened Star gave a delicately nervous shiver before reluctantly stepping inside.

'I know it's silly but I don't really like them,' she confessed only semi-untruthfully to Kyle as she stepped inside.

'It's a perfectly natural feeling,' he assured her as he followed her in and waited for her to tell him her floor number. 'I doubt there are many of us who actually enjoy being confined in such a small space, if we're honest about it.'

When the lift came to a halt at Star's floor Kyle politely stood back to allow her to precede him out of the lift before falling into step beside her.

Star deliberately waited until they were outside her bedroom door before starting to search her bag for her passkey, and then, when she did find it, she deliberately let it slip through her fingers so that Kyle had no option but to bend down to retrieve it for her, thus allowing her to close the small gap between them so that when he stood up again they were virtually standing body to body.

As she looked at his mouth Star deliberately let her own lips part slightly, her voice softly breathless as she thanked him for her key. She leaned forward, letting her body sway provocatively against his, her eyes starting to close on a small, whispered breath.

It was inevitable, of course, that he should respond to her, his head bending towards hers as he reached out to take hold of her.

It wasn't just triumph that she could feel as her small ploy worked, Star acknowledged. The pleasure warming her body was not purely that of victory. She could feel his body against her own now, satisfyingly male and hard-packed with muscle. His skin smelt clean and fresh and she was already anticipating how good it would be to give in to the feminine urge to bury her fingers in the thick darkness of his hair when they kissed. And she knew that he would kiss well. His mouth had already told her that. She looked at it now, not needing to fake the look of sensual appreciation in her eyes as she lifted them to meet his.

She would be generous in victory, she decided dizzily, very generous, when she showed him just how good it could be, when she made him admit that he wanted her—and she *would* make him admit it.

She saw the way his eyes changed as he felt the full warmth of her breasts pressing against his chest and a sharp thrill of arousal ran through her as she saw the dark burn of desire igniting his gaze.

'Kiss me,' she whispered compellingly to him as she finally closed the small space between her own mouth and his and placed her lips on his.

He responded immediately, as she had expected, his arms tightening around her, his mouth reacting to the soft pressure of hers whilst she teased him a little bit with delicate butterfly kisses which ended, as she had known they would, with his opening his mouth over hers.

She had been right about him being good, she decided dazedly several minutes later. It wasn't fiction any longer that she felt slightly light-headed and needed to cling to him for support, and there was certainly nothing faked about the way her heart was racing, nor the growing tumult of sensation threatening to flood her body.

She couldn't remember the last time a man had affected her so powerfully or so immediately. In fact, she

didn't think there had ever been such a time...nor such
a man. And she knew that he was equally affected. They
were standing body to body after all, and there was no
mistaking or concealing his own, very male arousal and
response to her, even if he had tried to move discreetly
away from her—but Star was perfectly well aware that
her own body was betraying *her* as flagrantly as his was
him.

The fluid fabric of her dress could not possibly conceal the taut peaks of her nipples, but Star was not
ashamed of nor embarrassed by her body's response to
him. Why should she be?

She was even tempted to lift his hand and place it on
her breast so that he could experience for himself the
effect he was having on her, but there was no need for
them to rush things. They had the whole night ahead of
them and there was something to be said for drawing
out the pleasure of mutual discovery and its even more
pleasurable culmination.

There was no doubt in Star's mind that his mouth
would feel every bit as good against her body as it did
against her lips and that when he finally placed it against
her naked breasts and slowly caressed each sensually
aroused peak the pleasure she would experience would
more than compensate for the control she was forcing
herself to exercise now.

And besides...

Besides, it had been a long time—a long, long time—
since she had last experienced something like this, since
she had last been held and kissed by a man who seemed
to read her mind and her desires so exactly that all she
wanted to do was cling to him and let his mouth...

With a tiny little moan, Star moved closer and opened
her mouth beneath his, inviting him to deepen his kiss
with the thrust of his tongue, her body quivering with
aching arousal as she waited for him to do so...and
waited...and waited. Confused, Star opened her eyes.

Kyle had stopped kissing her now and his hands were cupping her face.

As she read the message in his eyes, Star's own eyes widened, at first in disbelief and then in anger, her hands dropping to her sides as he kissed her lightly on the mouth once and then a second time a little more lingeringly. But even as she made to return to his arms he was gently releasing her, saying quietly but oh, so firmly, 'I'm sorry...'

Sorry... He was sorry! Star couldn't believe it.

Confused and wrought-up by the messages her body was sending her, Star couldn't control the sharp-toothed bite of her shocked chagrin and the dismay that followed it as she exclaimed, 'You're *sorry*!'

How dared he do this to her? How dared he hold her, touch her, *kiss* her as though...as though...

Struggling to contain and control her emotions, Star took a deep lungful of air, trying to find a suitably acerbic response to his unbelievable withdrawal. But all she could think of was how his body had felt against hers, how she could have sworn he wanted her, how she knew that he had been aroused and that men, in her experience of them, did follow up on that kind of arousal, especially when...especially with her...

As she looked in furious disbelief from his mouth— stiffening her body against the treacherous memory of just how good it had felt to have it moving against her own—and up to his eyes Star realised that the expression she could see in their navy blue depths was not one of male sexual triumph as she had expected but instead a totally unfamiliar mix of warmth and compassion.

Compassion... He felt *sorry* for her. How dared he...? How dared he?

Immediately her defensive reflexes, honed over the years until they were needle-sharp, sprang into action, her spine straightening, her head lifting, her eyes flashing a fierce message of warning and pride as she stepped

back from him and told him icily, with a disdainful
shrug, 'Don't be. After all, I'm hardly missing out on
the world's most exciting sexual experience, am I? You
aren't the only man to feel threatened and emasculated
by the strength and honesty of a woman's sexuality... I
suppose I should have realised what kind of man you
were when you tried to hide behind that claim that you
could only have sex with someone you "lurved",' she
taunted him mockingly. 'It's the classic get-out for men
like you, isn't it...?'

She gave him a falsely compassionate smile and
touched him contemptuously on the arm as she
added, 'We can't all be the same, of course. But it must
be hard, I know, for a man to admit that he's only got
a very low sex drive. Thanks for warning me about yours
before things went any further. There's nothing more
disappointing for a normal, healthy, sexually motivated
woman than a man who can't...whose libido doesn't
match hers...'

Before she turned away from him and swept into her
room Star paused to look tauntingly into his eyes, but,
to her surprise, instead of betraying the chagrin and anger she had expected—after all, no man could endure
having his masculinity, his sexuality called into question,
especially by a woman—he was just standing watching
her steadily.

The man was an idiot...a total blockhead. Star was still
fuming half an hour later as she slipped between the
cool, fresh sheets of her hotel bed. He had to be to have
behaved the way he had.

She knew that he had been turned on, aroused, when
they were sharing that passionate kiss; she had felt the
unmistakable hardness of his body against hers.

When sleep eluded her she thumped the pillow angrily, refusing to admit that it wasn't so much Kyle's
calm expression of his lack of any desire to take things

to their natural sexual conclusion that was keeping her sleepless and furious as her own unwanted excess of desire.

How could she, a sophisticated, experienced woman in her mid-twenties, who had had no trouble at all in remaining celibate for over two years, suddenly want one man so much that her body ached as painfully as though she had succumbed to a virulent fever?

With a small, fierce groan she closed her eyes angrily, willing herself to go to sleep. She had a busy day ahead of her tomorrow, starting with an early-morning meeting with Brad, and that was what she ought to be concentrating on, not some pathetic apology of a man whose claim to some hypothetical high moral ground was simply a cloak to conceal his real lack of libido.

It was just over half an hour's drive from the hotel downtown to the lakeside home that Kyle had bought when his distribution business had first become successful.

A little further up the lake and rather more isolated than Brad's home, the clapboard house had virtually been on the point of falling down when Kyle had bought it.

He had done most of the restoration work himself, enjoying the challenge of not only practically rebuilding the old house but also scouring the neighbourhood for the replacement materials he had needed to do so.

It had amused him the previous summer to be approached by the features editor of a local prestige publication who wanted to run a piece on the house and the restoration work he had done on it.

It hadn't just been his home that the features editor had shown an interest in either. She had been an attractive, vivacious brunette with a sensational sense of humour to match her equally sensational figure and Kyle had had to remind himself pretty sternly of the vow he had made to himself.

An ambitious college graduate, she had made it plain that all she was looking for was a summer romance before she headed for New York and fame. But he had done the New York thing and discovered that, after all, he was really a small-town guy at heart, with small-town values and beliefs and, if he was honest with himself, which he tried to be, happily content that that should be so.

Friends teased him about the fact that he lived alone in what was so obviously a family home, but he simply smiled good naturedly, laughing with them.

Only Kyle really knew how important his home was to him and how much he had felt in need of somewhere that was his own, of roots, of stability and continuity, after the confusion and pain of his early childhood.

Knowing that he had too much on his mind to sleep, he parked the car and walked down to the lake following the shoreline, his mouth quirking into a rueful smile as he recalled the angry insult that Star had flung at him outside her bedroom door.

If only she knew. Not since his turbulent teenage years had he experienced such an overwhelming surge of sexual desire.

Just standing there in the hotel corridor kissing her, he had already, in his imagination, removed her clothes, stroked the satiny softness of her skin, felt the soft feminine tremble of her body as he cupped the warm, full globes of her breasts, marvelling at the contrast between their creamy satin fullness and the dusky rose-brown of their areolae and the taut nipples that crested them, just as he had already felt the way she'd moved against him, her eyes closing, her body swaying and straining closer to his hands and mouth as he gave in to his desire to touch and taste the sweet femininity of her.

He knew exactly how it would be. How she would

cry out in sharp pleasure as he kissed the quivering softness of her throat and then moved lower over the creamy
slopes of her breasts and lower still until a taut nipple
was his captive, drawn into the hot suckle of his hungry
mouth, he equally its prisoner as he felt himself yield to
the sensual power of his desire for her.

Yes, it had been a long time since a woman had affected him so intensely, so overwhelmingly, so sexually…and so emotionally.

There had been a moment after he had released her
when he had looked into her eyes and seen beyond the
outraged anger of her pride to the hurt bewilderment
behind it and had had to fight with himself not to step
forward again and take her in his arms and hold her
there.

If he had done… If he had done, right now his body
wouldn't be aching so hard that he was practically grinding his teeth with the intensity of it. But there was more
to being a man than satisfying a sex urge… Much more,
even if Star Flower did not appear to think so.

One day he would… He had already turned round and
started to retrace his steps, but now abruptly he stopped
and stared out across the lake's deceptively placid sur-
face. One day he would what?

Right now he ought to be thinking of ways of calming
the situation. Tomorrow morning, when Brad formally
introduced him to Star and told her that they were going
to be working together in Britain, she wasn't going to
like it; she wasn't going to like it at all.

CHAPTER THREE

'AND one vital aspect which I'd particularly want you to focus on in any campaign is the reliability not just of our systems but, even more importantly, of their installation and maintenance.'

Star raised one eyebrow as she swiftly made a brief note of what Brad was saying to her. She had done her homework very thoroughly indeed before coming over to the States to meet with him and that homework had included interviews with those who had already had Brad's company's air-conditioning systems installed. A complaint from many of them had concerned the delays and problems that they had experienced in getting the systems installed and running efficiently.

'Is something wrong?' Brad asked her thoughtfully now, seeing that raised eyebrow.

'From what I've heard, there seems to be a problem with the installation and back-up system in Britain,' Star told him unhesitatingly. 'And, that being the case, I wouldn't have thought it was a good idea to focus any PR campaign in that particular direction.'

'We have had problems in that area,' Brad agreed, 'which is one of the reasons why I'm hiring you to come up with a campaign which will improve our image in that area...' He paused as his intercom buzzed, excusing himself to Star whilst he answered it.

'Yes, that's fine, Jan,' Star heard him saying warmly. 'Tell him to come right through.

'I am aware of the problems and I have taken steps

to correct them,' Brad continued to Star, 'and for that reason I've asked a friend and business associate of mine, who owns a highly successful business over here, to help us out by going over to Britain and seeing what he can do to improve things over there, so far as the installation and service side of things is concerned...

'I've actually asked him to call by this morning so that the two of you can meet. You'll like him. He's—' Brad broke off as the door opened. 'Ah, Kyle!' Star heard him exclaim warmly. 'Good... Come in and meet Star.'

'Star...' Brad began as Star fought to control her consternation.

But Kyle forestalled him, saying calmly, 'Star...Ms Flower and I have already introduced ourselves to one another.'

They might have introduced themselves to one another, as he had put it, but he had certainly made no mention of who exactly he was, nor of the fact that there was every chance that they were going to have to work together, Star fumed as she gave him a glitteringly insincere smile.

Now she understood what had motivated him last night. Quite plainly, knowing who she was, he had decided that he didn't want to become sexually involved with her, to allow her to have any kind of upper hand or control of the situation when he knew that they were going to have to work together.

She, regrettably, had not had the benefit of that particular piece of information, and if she had done...

'I'm sure that the two of you are going to work very well together,' she heard Brad saying.

She could feel Kyle looking at her, almost willing her to look directly at him, but she refused to do so, keeping her gaze fixed rigidly instead on a point several feet away whilst she said with as much calm as she could muster, 'I understood that I would be working with Tim

Burbridge.' She was referring to a relative of Claire's. 'I thought he was in charge of the British side of your distribution network.'

'Yes, he is,' Brad agreed, 'but, as you've already mentioned yourself, there have been problems in establishing the standard of installation and back-up service we pride ourselves on giving our customers, and as Tim would be the first to admit, whilst he has no problem selling the units to customers, he is finding it difficult to recruit the right kind of technical people to follow through from his sales, and that's where Kyle comes in.

'Not only does Kyle have a firsthand knowledge of just how our units should be installed and maintained but he has also built up States-side the very best installation and service team we have ever used.'

Star's mouth twisted in a slightly cynical smile as she listened to Brad singing Kyle's praises.

'The British employee's psyche and attitude to work is not necessarily the same as an American's,' she announced coolly. 'What works here in America will not necessarily work in Britain,' she said challengingly, looking directly at Kyle for the first time, the warning look in her eyes telling him that what had happened last night was now in the past and that he would be a very foolhardy man indeed if he tried to make any capital out of it now.

'That's true,' he agreed, answering her, 'and I appreciate that there will be certain...cultural difficulties to overcome...'

'Which is, hopefully, one of the ways in which you will be able to help Kyle find the right approach,' Brad intervened.

Star's eyebrows lifted as she pointed out coolly, 'I'm a PR consultant, not a sociologist.'

'Yes, but you've already highlighted our main area of weakness,' Brad was quick to tell her, 'and I suspect you're far too intelligent and independent a woman not to have formed certain conclusions and views on how the problem can best be resolved.'

What Brad was saying was no less than the truth but his praise immediately made Star feel wary and suspicious. Men did not, in her experience, praise women unless they wanted something in return.

Brad and Kyle were obviously close friends and she wondered suspiciously if it was, perhaps, in their minds to place any blame for any potential failure on Kyle's part to achieve the same success in Britain as he had done in the States on her shoulders, or rather on the shoulders of her PR campaign. It was not, after all, unheard of for men to use such tactics—gamesmanship, they called it; plain underhand was a more honest description in her book.

'It's my job to promote the company from a PR point of view,' she told Brad firmly. 'Or at least that's what I understood the contract I signed earlier to say.'

'Yes, of course,' Brad agreed politely. He looked slightly puzzled, causing Star to wonder if she might have misjudged him and even been guilty of a little paranoia, but where men were concerned a woman couldn't be too careful, she reminded herself. Look at the way Kyle had withheld from her the fact that he already knew that they were going to be seeing each other again.

'I know you're flying back home today,' Brad told her, 'but Claire wondered if you'd time to have lunch with her and Sally before you left. She said to tell you that she'd pick you up at your hotel at noon.'

There was really no way Star could refuse. Sally was, after all, her closest and oldest friend and during her turbulent teenage years her home and her stepmother had provided Star with the kind of warmth and stability that her own home life had lacked.

Ten minutes later, as she left Brad's office, she couldn't bring herself to look directly at Kyle. Gritting her teeth, she walked past him, her head held high.

All right, so he might very well have stolen a march on her and was no doubt right now enjoying that sensation—enjoying knowing that he had rejected her, enjoying the superiority and sense of power he probably felt that gave him—but she was damned if she was going to give him the satisfaction of letting him see that she was aware of his triumph.

'Come on, the champagne's already on ice,' Sally announced, pouncing on Star as she walked into the hotel foyer. 'You did sign the contract, didn't you?' she asked, frowning slightly as she saw how grimly preoccupied Star looked.

'Yes, I signed the contract,' Star confirmed.

'Star, what is it, what's wrong?' Sally began, confused. 'I thought you'd be over the moon. You said yourself that this would be the biggest contract you'd had; you were so excited about it and—'

'It's nothing... Just a bit of jet lag,' Star lied, forcing herself to smile. What was the point, after all, in advertising her sense of ill-usage? Sally wouldn't really understand. She had never shared Star's feelings about the perfidious nature of the male sex.

'Claire's waiting for us in the dining room,' Sally explained, taking hold of Star's arm as she added, 'No, not this way. We've got our own private dining room courtesy of Brad. He's a darling, isn't he? But then American men *are* sweeties, aren't they? Just look at Kyle...' Sally closed her eyes and gave a small, ecstatic sigh of deeply feminine approval.

'If it wasn't for Chris, I think I could fall for Kyle in a big way—a *very* big way,' she emphasised. 'He's got that something about him that tells you you could rely on him utterly and completely, hasn't he? You just *know* that he's the kind of man who would always be able to get a taxi and produce an umbrella when it rains.'

'Oh, yes, irresistible,' Star replied sarcastically, trying

to hold onto her temper as she listened to Sally eulogising on Kyle's supposed virtues.

'You don't like him, do you?' Sally guessed. 'But Star—'

'Personally, I prefer my men a little less homey and a little more sexy. All right, then, a lot more sexy,' she told Sally recklessly. 'And—'

'Oh, but Kyle *is* sexy,' Sally interrupted her to protest. 'He's very sexy,' she insisted. 'Anyway, enough about him. How did your dinner date with that guy go last night?'

Star murmured something non-committal, her expression clearly revealing that she didn't want to talk about it.

'Look, Star,' Sally said gently as she saw the familiar stubbornness tighten Star's mouth and recognised the look in her eyes, 'I know how you feel about men and I *do* understand, but just because your father—'

'Just because my father what?' Star demanded dangerously.

Sally gave a small sigh and tried again.

'Not all men are the same. Look at Chris...and Brad...and James... And Kyle is—'

'The kind of man who claims he can only have sex with a woman he feels emotionally bonded to,' Star interrupted her savagely, and added vehemently, 'He's lying. I know it and I mean to prove it, to make him—'

She stopped speaking, abruptly aware that she had been letting things get out of control and allowing herself to be swamped by her emotions.

'Star,' she heard Sally appealing softly, but she refused to respond to her friend's plea, turning her head away when Sally suggested gently, 'I can see that you and Kyle obviously haven't quite hit it off, but don't you think you could be overreacting a little bit...? He really is one of the most genuine men...people I have ever met and everyone else, including Brad, has a very

high regard for him; he says he's the most honest and
straightforward man he's ever known—very highly mor-
ally principled and completely a man of his word, whilst,
at the same time, always having the ability to see the
other person's point of view and to treat them compassionately.'

'Brad would think that—he's another man,' Star
sneered, her body stiffening in rejection of what Sally
was trying to tell her.

But, even whilst her body language was challenging
Sally to continue to oppose her, inwardly her stomach
had started to churn in a long-familiar mixture of pain
and fear made highly toxic by a generous inclusion of
panic as she fought to hold onto her beliefs and her self
control.

A long, long time ago she had first experienced that
same volatile cocktail of destructive and painful
emotions when listening to her mother denouncing her
father. Then she had fought fiercely to deny and reject
what her mother was saying, convinced that she was
wrong, that her father loved them—that he would never
leave them, and she had been wrong.

But she was not wrong now. She was not wrong about
Kyle.

And somehow she would find a way of proving, not
just to herself but also to those like Sally who doubted
her judgement, that she *was* right.

Somehow she would find a way of exposing Kyle's
hypocrisy for what it was. It would be her own personal
crusade, her own private war.

'Well, perhaps Kyle just isn't your type,' Sally was
saying diplomatically, obviously anxious to smooth
things over. 'According to Brad he's an idealist and a
romantic. It's a shame that there isn't anyone special in
his life,' she added musingly. 'I suppose the kind of
woman that would be most likely to appeal to him is

someone soft and gentle, someone he could cherish and protect, and that's not you at all, is it?'

'No, it certainly isn't,' Star agreed shortly.

'Well, we'll just have to see if we can't find him someone suitable at home,' Sally chattered on. 'Any suggestions?'

'Sally, I'm a PR consultant, not a dating agency or a marriage bureau,' Star snapped. 'I'm sorry,' she said when she saw Sally biting her lip. 'I'm just feeling a bit on edge.'

'A *bit*!' Sally exclaimed, feelingly. 'When Claire told me that Brad was definitely going to offer you a contract I thought you'd be on top of the world. After all, you've talked of nothing else for weeks.'

'I know,' Star agreed contritely.

What Sally had said was true. When she had first discussed the possibility of organising a PR campaign with Brad and Tim in England she had told Sally that if Brad did give her a contract it would be the biggest step forward in her solo professional career that she was ever likely to take.

She had worked on big accounts before but only as part of a team, and her clients now were, in the main, small, fledgling businesses very much like her own. The mere fact that she would be working with such a male-dominated business would also add the kind of gravitas to her business portfolio that she might otherwise have spent years trying to achieve. It wasn't just a matter of the additional income she would earn, it was the fact that doors to other business opportunities would open for her if she mounted a successful nationwide campaign for Brad's company.

She knew that she had a strong flair for her work and that her ideas were innovative and fresh. To have Brad confirm that, not just verbally as he had done this morning but materially as well in offering her a contract, should have filled her with exultation and pride, but instead all she could think of was the fact that Kyle wasn't going to be an unwanted memory that she could leave behind her when she flew home but a very intrusive presence in her life, and that no matter how hard she tried to ignore him...

Star started to frown. There were always two ways of looking at a problem: one was to see it as an obstacle to be overcome, something that used up valuable energy and time, the other was to look at it in a more positive light, to turn it into something that could be used to one's own advantage.

She remembered how seethingly angry she had been at the way that Kyle had managed to turn the tables on her and how much it had galled her knowing that she would have to walk away, allowing him to cling to his false piety and morality, secretly laughing at her, but the fact that he was going to be working in Britain, even if only for a short time, meant that she would have a second chance to prove herself right, to make good her angry claim to Sally that he was not the knight in shining armour that Sally believed.

'I'm sorry if I don't seem very enthusiastic,' she apologised to Sally, acknowledging that. 'I suppose I still haven't quite taken it all in.'

'Well, it's only natural that you'll worry a little bit about it now that the initial euphoria's worn off,' Sally comforted her. 'But at least you'll have Kyle on hand to turn to... I know that Tim's a dear but he isn't exactly... He doesn't...' She paused and made a small face.

'I doubt very much that I shall have much contact with Kyle,' Star returned crisply as Sally indicated the door which led to their private dining room. 'After all, it is Tim Burbridge who is in charge of the distribution side of things and Kyle's role is only peripheral to my work, so I—'

'Oh, but Tim won't—' Sally began, only to break off

as her stepmother opened the door and exclaimed warmly,

'Star, my dear! Come on in!'

By the time she boarded her home-bound flight Star's mood had been mellowed by the delicious surprise lunch that Claire had given for her and the equally delicious vintage champagne she had consumed.

She settled herself in her seat and closed her eyes, opening them again when she heard an attractive male voice enquiring, 'Er...mind if I sit here next to you?'

Thoughtfully Star subjected him to a brief inspection. He was certainly good-looking but for some reason she felt less than enthusiastic at the thought of enduring several hours of heavily seductive flirtation.

Refusing to return his smile, Star claimed untruthfully, 'I'm sorry, that seat's already taken by my mother.'

Whilst Star was crossing the Atlantic, Kyle was standing at the window of his office in one of the town's most prestigious blocks, staring frowningly through it.

It would be a simple enough matter to pick up the phone and tell Brad that he had changed his mind; that he couldn't, after all, help him and fly out to Britain; it was, after all, what all his instincts warned him to do—but he already knew that he wasn't going to make that phone call, that he couldn't bring himself to go back on his agreement to help Brad.

He had known, even before they had met this morning, that Star would not forgive him easily either for last night or for withholding from her the fact that he'd known that they would be working together—two strikes against him already. One more and he would be totally and completely out of the game, which, where a woman like Star was concerned, was surely his safer and saner option, he comforted himself.

So why, then, was he so reluctant to embrace it...? As reluctant, in fact, as Star assumed he had been to embrace her—assumed so erroneously, so very, very erroneously. If only she knew...

Thank the Lord she didn't, he mused; he was going to have enough problems to contend with as it was.

CHAPTER FOUR

IN THE fortnight following her return from America Star was too busy professionally to have any time to spend working on her campaign to prove that Kyle was not the saintly, exemplary male that he liked to pretend he was.

Her hectic schedule culminated in an overnight stay in London whilst she attended a trade fair with one of her clients—a young and very talented interior designer. Having persuaded a highly acclaimed local builder of prestige houses to allow Lindsay a free hand in the interior design of one of his show houses, Star had then used her contacts to get the house featured in the new homes supplement of one of the national dailies.

As a result, not only had the builder sold every single one of the houses on his small, exclusive development but Lindsay had also been inundated with new commissions and couldn't heap enough praise on Star for what she had done.

'At least let me redesign your flat...as a bonus,' she begged Star now as they travelled home together in Star's car, Star at the wheel.

'I'm very tempted,' Star acknowledged, 'but there's the problem of where I would live and, more important, where I would work in the meantime.'

'Mmm...I'd forgotten for a moment that you work from home,' Lindsay said and added curiously, 'Wouldn't you prefer to rent an office somewhere and keep your work separate from your private life?'

'My work *is* my private life,' Star told her and meant

it. 'And I can see no point in passing the expensive and unnecessary overheads involved in maintaining a fully equipped office on to my clients when I can work just as easily from home and be there on hand whenever they need me. My flat has two good-sized double bedrooms and it was no hardship to convert one of them into an office.'

'Mmm…Carey's built your flat, didn't they?' Lindsay asked her.

'Yes,' Star agreed. 'That was how I first came into contact with them. I went to look at the site when I first saw the flats advertised. At that stage Frank Carey was planning to build one-bedroom apartments plus some slightly larger flats with one double bedroom and a box room… I pointed out to him that so far as most people were concerned a box room served only one purpose and that was for the storage of junk and that he'd sell the properties far more easily if he cut down on the number of flats by one and increased the floor space of all the others to include a good-sized double bedroom.

'He refused to listen to me at first…'

Frank Carey was a man in his early sixties who had been in the building trade since he left school and was, it had to be said, just ever so slightly tinged with an old-fashioned attitude towards women, to put it politely. Lindsay, with her own experience of just how stubborn he could be, asked Star curiously, 'How did you manage to get him to change his mind?'

Star grinned at her.

'I persuaded twenty of my friends to make interested noises about the rest of the flats with a proviso that he increased the size of the box room.'

'And it worked…? He didn't suspect?' Lindsay asked, awed.

Star laughed.

'Oh, yes, he guessed what I was up to all right, but in the end he gave in, and out of the twenty people who originally showed interest in the flats he eventually got seven sales.'

Whilst Lindsay stared at her in round-eyed respect, Star gave a small, self-deprecatory shrug and told her, 'That, like getting your designs featured in the national press, was more good luck than anything else. However, when Frank eventually offered me a good discount on my own flat, I didn't turn him down.'

'I suppose *I* ought to be thinking of moving to somewhere smaller and more easily manageable,' Lindsay acknowledged dolefully.

'It's definitely over, then—your marriage?' Star queried.

She knew that Lindsay and her husband had split up several months earlier. Her husband, from what Lindsay had said and from what Star had read between the stilted lines of explanation that she had been given, was apparently unable to accept the sudden success of his wife's business and the fact that she was now the major breadwinner in their small household.

Star had only met Miles Reynolds briefly. He was, according to Lindsay, a hugely gifted and underappreciated set designer. Star had found him sullen and inclined to try to put down his long-suffering wife.

It had been his decision to move out, because, or so he'd complained, it was obvious that Lindsay's business success had gone to her head and now meant more to her than he did.

Lindsay had begged him to come back but Star had urged her not to give in to his emotional blackmail and to leave him to stew in his own sulks.

Now it seemed that the marriage was definitely over.

'You'll have to take care, when you file for divorce, to protect your ownership of the business,' Star warned her now.

'Divorce?' Lindsay gave her a shocked look. 'Oh, no, I don't think...' She lapsed back into silence, unwilling to admit to Star, whose views of marriage and men she now knew very well, that she still loved her husband and that there were times when, despite the fact that she knew he was behaving both childishly and selfishly, she missed him and ached for him so desperately that she was quite willing to give up the business completely just to have him back.

Only her common sense kept her from telling him so, and she knew that Star would be as little able to understand how she could continue to love him and to accept him as he was, faults and all, as Miles was to understand how important the stability afforded by her own business success was to her and her hopes for the future, for the family she had hoped they would one day have.

'Remember,' Star warned Lindsay as she dropped her off outside her front door, 'no more freebies, no matter *who* asks for them; you don't need them any more...'

'No,' Lindsay agreed meekly, bit her lip. Then she temporised, 'Well, only the sitting room at the new centre they're opening in town for the over-sixties. They deserve it, Star,' she protested when she saw Star's expression. 'They've worked hard all their lives and they deserve a bit of comfort and care now; besides, I've already promised.'

Giving her a dry look, Star put her car back in gear. Some people were just too soft for their own good, she thought.

Once home, as she went through her post, she reran her answering machine to listen to her messages. Most of them were non-urgent; she tensed as she listened to one from her mother detailing the most recent instalment in the saga of her current romance. Star sighed as she heard the indignation mounting in her mother's voice as she described the confrontation with her friend over the discovery that she, Star's mother, was deeply embroiled in an affair with the friend's still-not-quite-twenty-one-year-old son.

Shaking her head, Star wound the tape on. She would call her mother later.

There was a message from Tim saying that he wanted to discuss with her the story-boards that she had dropped off with him the week before.

These outlined the basics of a possible nationwide advertisement that she had thought of running to bring the company's product into the public eye.

What she had in mind was to use a similar theme to that of a certain very successful coffee ad, by planning a set of ongoing ads that linked together in instalment form to make a story.

The first depicted the overheated atmosphere in an industrial setting without the benefit of any air-conditioning, coupled with the arrival of a visitor from a competitive business which had the benefit of Brad's air conditioning units. To inject a little humour into the situation Star's story-boards had depicted several of the extras in various states of undress. She intended to follow the first ad up with a second showing the coolly competent visitor offering the name of their air-conditioning supplier, but his rival deciding to use a cheaper and less reliable X brand.

Into the resultant chaos would walk the cool, important female buyer whose business both firms were competing for, at which point the X brand units would break down, allowing the user of Brad's air-conditioning to sweep her off to his own cool and well-ordered factory where the deal could be agreed in true ad fashion with a clinch. At this point there would be a tongue in cheek stating that there was only one situation where an efficient air-conditioning system could be too efficient. The elegant female buyer would purr, 'And is this how you turn it down...? Ah, yes... Goodness, it seems hot in here...' Her hand would reach out to stop the man's from turning it up again as she whispered, 'I have a better idea,' and reached behind her to undo the halter-neck tie of her top.

So far Star had only presented Tim with the first segment of the story, hoping to whet his appetite for the rest.

What she hoped to persuade him to do was to agree to a nationwide TV campaign. She had done her costings and was convinced that a successful campaign would fully justify the costs involved.

It wasn't just Tim whom she would have to convince, though, she reminded herself; it was Brad as well.

Having checked her diary, she rang and left a message on Tim's answering machine to confirm that the appointment he had suggested for the following morning was convenient.

As she left home the following morning, Star noticed that the 'TO LET' board for the flat adjacent to her own had disappeared, and she wondered briefly what her new neighbour would be like before concentrating on more important matters.

They were having an exceptionally good summer and the town was full of people in casual, brightly coloured clothes.

Star, in contrast, was quite formally dressed in a subtle beige pleated silk skirt and a contrasting cream silk long-line sleeveless top. Her skin tanned well despite the colour of her hair, going a warm peach rather than a deep bronze, and she was sardonically aware of the interest that she was creating amongst the male motorists at the garage when she stopped for petrol.

Resolutely refusing to make eye contact with the most persistent of them, she went to pay for her petrol. The garage sold basic groceries along with sweets and ice cream, and, whilst she was waiting to be served, on impulse, Star reached into the freezer for an ice cream—

the kind that came on a stick and was covered in chocolate.

Having unwrapped it and disposed of the wrapper on her way back to her car, she had just unlocked the door when she heard a male voice to one side of her. 'Very sexy... It's really turning me on and making me hot, watching you suck that.'

Inwardly furious, but refusing to be intimidated or to show any kind of embarrassment or self-consciousness, Star turned round and looked coldly at him.

Middle-aged and besuited, he looked for all the world like the 'Mr Average' respectable family man he no doubt claimed that he was, and Star had no doubt that his wife would immediately have denied the very idea that her husband could behave so offensively.

He was still leering at her and now he was looking at her breasts, Star observed, and she removed the ice cream from her mouth and told him with acid venom as she pushed the melting ice cream onto the front of his shirt, 'Here—perhaps this will help you to cool down.'

Let him explain that to his wife if he dared, she thought.

As she spun round on her heel and got into her car she noticed that the garage forecourt was now empty apart from the obnoxious man's saloon and a sturdy four-wheel drive which had drawn up at the other side of the pumps.

As she drove off she glanced at her watch. She had plenty of time to make her appointment with Tim. Mentally she rehearsed the argument that she had prepared to counter the objections she suspected he would have to such a high-profile and expensive campaign.

From his hired four-wheel drive, Kyle watched thoughtfully as Star slammed her car door and started her engine.

He had seen her crossing the forecourt as he had

driven into the garage and had been on the point of walking over to speak to her when he had witnessed her confrontation with the other driver and overheard what he had said to her.

There was, in his book, no possible excuse for the other man's behaviour, but he wondered what it was about certain people that caused them to attract to themselves situations which could only reaffirm their distorted views and suspicions of others. Was it, perhaps, due to some powerful cosmic force which had as yet to be scientifically identified? he mused fancifully as he went to pay for his own petrol. He doubted it.

He had been in Britain less than a week and had already discovered that although the climate was reputed to lack a certain warmth its people did not. Sally and Chris in particular had made him very welcome. Star, he suspected, would greet his arrival with considerably less enthusiasm.

'I don't think Star realises that you're actually going to be taking over from Tim,' Sally had confided to him the previous evening when she and Chris had invited him round for dinner. 'I know she can seem a little difficult—' she had begun in defence of her friend, but Chris had interrupted her acerbically.

'She's a man-hater, a real ball-breaker...'

'Oh, Chris, that's not fair,' Sally had reproved her husband. 'Star had an awfully difficult childhood,' she had told Kyle. 'She adored her father and the way he rejected her was so cruel...

'Well, you already know the story,' she'd finished awkwardly as Chris had given a derisive snort.

Then Chris had demanded, 'Can we please talk about something a little more pleasant than your socially dysfunctional friend?' He had proceeded to tell Kyle, 'She's like one of those spiders—the ones that destroy their mates after they've been bedded by them. And they talk about men being sexually predatory...'

'Chris, that's not fair,' Sally had protested defensively.

'Oh, come on,' Chris had retorted, then had quickly explained to Kyle Star's complete rejection of the idea that catching Sally's wedding bouquet could alter her decision never to marry or commit herself to a relationship.

'It's only because she's so desperately afraid of being hurt again the way her father hurt her, don't you agree?' Sally had appealed to Kyle.

'Yes,' he'd confirmed. 'You've only got to look at the animal world to see how often the need for self-protection leads to the masking of fear by an outward show of aggression.'

He mentally recalled that conversation now, and about the way Star had crushed the ice-cold remnant of her bitten ice cream against the obnoxious man's shirt.

As she waited in Tim's outer office, Star noticed that several changes had been made since she had last seen it—all of them an improvement, she noted approvingly as she observed how the pile of untidy, ancient magazines on the coffee-table had been removed and replaced by fresh, glossy ones and how, in fact, the whole waiting area had been changed around and now had far more comfortable, up-market furnishings, plus a self-service coffee and cold drinks machine and a TV screen showing a video of the American factory, including various technical specifications and details of the air conditioning units they made.

There was even, Star saw with some surprise, a display of fresh flowers, and the lighting seemed better, less harsh and yet at the same time giving more light.

Tim's middle-aged secretary-cum-receptionist smiled as she saw Star studying her surroundings and commented, 'Quite an improvement...'

'Very much so,' Star agreed, and glanced at her watch

before asking, 'Do I have time for a cup of coffee before
I see Tim or...?'

'Oh, no, it won't be—'

The other woman broke off as the door to the inner
office opened and a well-remembered American voice
announced calmly, 'Star, it's good to see you again.
Won't you please come through...?'

Kyle! Star stood up warily.

'My appointment was with Tim...' she began challengingly, but Kyle was already taking hold of her arm
and drawing her into the inner office, leaving her with
no alternative but to go with him.

Immediately they were inside, as he turned to close
the door, she shook herself free of his hold and demanded, 'Where's Tim?'

'On leave,' Kyle responded quietly.

'On leave...?' Star stared at him. 'For how long?'

'It hasn't been decided yet. Brad felt that he would
benefit from a month, possibly six weeks...'

Six weeks!

'So who's taking his place whilst he's away?' Star
asked, but she suspected that she already knew the answer.

Even so, her heart plummeted as she heard Kyle say,
'I am.'

'But that's not possible; you can't be,' she protested,
an unfamiliar sensation burning her face as she realised
that her own gaucherie had made her colour up betrayingly. '*You* aren't employed by the company,' she
amended. 'You're *not* a salesman. I was told that you
were coming over here to sort out the technical side of
things. If I'd known that I'd...' She paused.

Kyle told her calmly, 'I'm sorry if you think you've
been misled; it certainly wasn't intentional...'

'But you knew before you came here that you were
going to be taking over from Tim?'

'Standing in for him, yes,' Kyle corrected her. He

paused and frowned slightly before continuing. 'I don't want to break any confidences but I'm sure that Tim wouldn't mind you knowing that the reason he's taking this period of extended leave is because he wants to update his management skills. On Brad's recommendation he's flying out to the US next week to take several courses at a specialised and very highly acclaimed personal development centre over there.'

'I see. I can't understand why Brad didn't tell me any of this before I signed the contract.'

'Perhaps he thought it wasn't important,' Kyle told her.

Behind him Star caught sight of her story-boards. Shrugging aside her anger at being caught off guard by Kyle's unexpected disclosures, she gestured towards them and said curtly, 'I'd better take those with me. Obviously the PR campaign will have to be put on hold now until Tim returns.'

'Why should you think that? On the contrary,' Kyle corrected her with maddening authority, 'Brad is keen for it to go ahead as quickly as possible. However...' he paused and looked from Star's angry face to the story-boards behind him '...whilst I can see the direction you're planning on taking with the campaign, I do have several problems with what you're proposing.'

Stonily Star glared at him. She had anticipated having one or two small tussles with Tim over the campaign, primarily over the ambitiousness and cost of what she was planning rather than anything else, but she had been reasonably confident of persuading him to add the weight of his consent to what she wanted to do when she ultimately put her proposal forward to Brad.

'If you're worried about the cost...' she began, but Kyle shook his head, not allowing her to continue.

'The cost isn't an issue at this juncture, but what does concern me is the degree of sexual stereotyping and the smutty, even pornographic slant to the ads. At home this kind of sexual innuendo, and indeed harassment, would never get past the censors and I—'

Star couldn't believe her ears.

'You're crazy,' she interrupted him angrily. 'There is nothing smutty about my work, and as for it being *pornographic*... How dare you suggest...? Might I remind you that my campaign is targeting the British market—a market which you are not, after all, familiar with? I can assure you that my campaign would have no problems with the censors here, and, as a matter of fact, a recent national campaign run on similar lines for another product has—'

'The coffee campaign,' Kyle interrupted her grimly. 'Yes, I know. I may not as yet be familiar with the British market, but I have been doing my research. That campaign, so far as I have seen, did not portray semi-naked male and female bodies in poses which might be considered more suitable for a crude seaside postcard.'

Star stared at him, almost too furious to be able to give vent to the angry words jamming her throat. 'My campaign has been carefully planned and thought out and is directed at a specific target market. It's a parody; it expresses tongue-in-cheek humour. It's a joke...'

'A joke? To portray a group of hard-working men stripping off to be taunted and mocked by their female colleagues? Would *you* think it a joke if the roles were reversed and it was a group of women removing their clothes to be leered at and catcalled by their male co-workers...?'

Star had heard enough.

'Oh, for goodness' sake!' she exclaimed, darting behind him to start gathering together her story-boards, her face flushed with fury.

'Don't think I don't know why you're doing this,' she told him cuttingly. 'I bet you just couldn't wait to get over here and start making things difficult for me, could you? Don't think I don't know that this is your way of getting back at me because your male ego couldn't take the fact that—'

'That what?' Kyle challenged her, his eyes suddenly so steely and compelling that Star found herself unable to drag her own gaze away from them. 'That I declined to take you up on your offer of sex? Hasn't anyone ever told you that the male animal likes to do his own hunting?'

'You claimed that you were different from other men,' Star reminded him, valiantly fighting back.

'No, I didn't say that,' Kyle corrected her. 'A psychiatrist would have a field day with you, you really are a textbook case. The young girl-child, abandoned and rejected by her father, who grows up to become a man-hater as a means of rejecting and separating herself from her pain. It even shows up in your work. Don't you *ever* get tired of it, Star? Don't you *ever* want a holiday from finding new ways to punish and ridicule the male sex?'

'My personal feelings have nothing to do with my work,' Star denied.

No one had ever spoken so forthrightly to her, or so brutally. So much for the chivalrous nature that Sally had insisted Kyle possessed.

'And neither have mine,' Kyle informed her quietly.

Their glances locked, and Star discovered to her chagrin that she was the first to look away.

For all his apparent amiability there was something as tough as hardened steel inside Kyle. Something...some belief in himself that he would not allow anyone to breach.

She wasn't going to give up so easily, though. She was convinced that her campaign would work. The trouble with Kyle was that he didn't understand the British psyche, the British sense of humour.

If necessary she would take her work to a higher authority, consult Brad direct... Either that or wait until Tim came back.

Drawing herself up to her full height, she glared haughtily at Kyle, burning him to cinders with the full furnace-blast of her contempt as she told him, 'I think, in the circumstances, it would be better if I put the campaign on hold until Tim returns. I can't—'

'No.'

'No...?' Star stared at him.

'Oh, I know what you're thinking,' Kyle told her. 'You think you can wheedle your way round Tim and get him to give his agreement to your proposals, but it won't work. Brad is anxious to get things moving as quickly as possible. He's given me the authority to take on board any extra help I think I might need in doing that if necessary.'

Any *extra* help. Star gave him a suspicious, narrow-eyed look. Was he threatening to go over her head and employ someone else to run the PR campaign?

'I have a contract,' she reminded him, just in case he had forgotten.

'Indeed,' Kyle agreed blandly, 'and I think if you read it you will discover that there are certain time clauses in it and certain contractual agreements which include the right of the company's representatives to veto your work...

'I do understand how you feel about my sex, Star,' Kyle added, more gently, 'and why you're letting your prejudices distort reality... Have you ever thought that counselling might help you to get things more into perspective, to let go of the past and—?'

'Go to hell,' Star told him rudely, picking up her work, her muscles straining against its weight as she manoeuvred herself towards the door.

When she reached it she turned back and looked at Kyle, determined not to let him have the last word or to feel that he had vanquished her in any way...*any* way!

'I don't care what you say, Kyle, you *are* just like all the rest of your sex—quite happy to cheat and lie, to deceive and hurt people, to do *anything* just as long as it allows you to do what you want to do—and I'm not deceived. I know what you're really like and I'm going to prove it to everyone else as well...'

Kyle had started to frown as he listened to her passionately angry outburst, looking not at her any longer but down at his desk. Only when she had finished did he raise his head again, his expression unreadable as he commented calmly, 'I see. So it's war, then, I take it...?'

'To the death,' Star vowed, and meant it.

CHAPTER FIVE

STAR was still fuming over Kyle's criticism of her campaign when she arrived home, and carrying the heavy story-boards upstairs to her second-floor flat did not help to improve her temper.

The communal landing which she shared with the other residents was not really designed to accommodate a woman of five feet six and weighing just a tad over eight stone plus two unwieldy, rigid pieces of board just that bit too deep to fit comfortably under her arm and too long to fit within her arm-span, and Star cursed under her breath as she banged her elbow on the wall.

She knew, of course, that it would have made much more sense for her to carry the boards upstairs singly instead of trying to move them both together, but she was still so infuriated by what Kyle had said to her that she just wasn't in the mood for behaving logically.

Once inside her own flat she inspected her elbow and grimaced as she realised that she had broken the skin. By tomorrow she would have a terrific bruise there—one of the penalties of her particular type of skin colouring, something else to count as a black mark against Kyle. Well, he wasn't the final authority and she would show him that *she* wasn't going to let him push her around. Quickly she looked up Brad's number, her fingers curling impatiently around the receiver, her voice crisply firm as she asked the telephonist who answered her call for Brad.

'I'm sorry,' the girl apologised, 'but I'm afraid he isn't available.'

When Star asked when he would be available and learned that Brad had taken Claire on a honeymoon trip sailing round the Virgin Islands, she thanked the girl and replaced the receiver.

No wonder Kyle had felt so confident about rejecting her work. He must have known that she wouldn't be able to go over his head to Brad.

She frowned as she heard her doorbell ring, and went to open the door.

Sally was standing outside and her eyebrows lifted questioningly as she asked, 'What's wrong?'

'I've just been trying to ring Brad,' Star told her. 'But he isn't there.'

'No, he and Claire are spending some time sailing around the Virgin Islands,' Sally confirmed. 'Lucky things... What did you want him for?' she enquired curiously, her attention distracted by the story-boards propped up against the wall. 'Are these for the campaign?' she asked Star interestedly. 'May I have a look or—?'

'Go ahead,' Star told her curtly.

'Mmm...*very* sexy,' Sally commented after she had studied them.

'Sexy? According to Kyle they're sex*ist*,' Star told her bitterly.

'He doesn't like them?' Sally asked sympathetically.

'He doesn't like *me*,' Star corrected her grimly. 'If I'd known that I was going to have to work so closely with him...' She pushed her fingers into her hair angrily.

'God, when I think how he must have been smirking to himself there in Brad's office, knowing that he was coming over here to take over from Tim and knowing, as well, that *I* didn't know. It wouldn't have mattered what kind of campaign I'd come up with; he would have rejected it.

'My campaign *is* good, Sally. I know it will work...'

'Mmm...well, couldn't you perhaps compromise a little...perhaps have just a little less emphasis on the...?'

She made a sketchy gesture in the direction of the
story-boards, causing Star to demand suspiciously,
'What are you trying to say—that *you* think he's
right...that *you* agree with him...?'

'No...of course not. I was just meaning that you could
perhaps meet him halfway and—'

'Give in to him, you mean. Pander to his male ego.
Let him think that he's *won*. Never!' Star told her
fiercely. 'Men are all the same,' she proclaimed bitterly.

Sally sighed.

'Star, isn't it time you let go of the past?' she suggested gently. 'Kyle was saying only the other night
that—'

'You were talking about *me* to *him*?' Star pounced on
her words, her face suddenly flushing angrily. 'What
were you saying? What did he say?' she demanded per-
emptorily.

'No, Star, it wasn't—' Sally protested, but Star
wouldn't let her finish.

'No, don't tell me. I don't want to know. I don't care
what he thinks about me or—'

'Look,' Sally cut in quickly, 'I only came round to
tell you that we're having a barbecue next weekend so
that we can introduce Kyle to a few people. It will be
lonely for him living over here and you remember what
I was saying about trying to find someone nice for
him...? Well, what about Lindsay? She's on her own
now, isn't she? And she'd be perfect for him. She's such
a wonderful home-maker and so sweet and gentle, and
now that her marriage is over—'

'It isn't over,' Star snapped. 'They're only separated,
not divorced.'

She had no idea why the thought of Lindsay as a
potential partner for Kyle should make her feel so...

so...so intensely antagonistic—probably because she disliked him so much herself.

'You will be able to make it, won't you?' Sally was asking her. 'I know it's short notice but—'

'No, I won't,' Star told her shortly, and refused to meet Sally's eyes as she told her, 'I...I'm going to see Mother. I owe her a visit and—'

'It's all right; I understand,' Sally told her quietly. 'I'd better go; I'm going to visit a friend who's just had a baby boy. He's so sweet and everyone who meets him just adores him...even Chris. I think he's beginning to come round to the idea of us starting our own family...'

Star was surprised to find her eyes stinging with hot tears after Sally had said goodbye.

She knew that Sally had not believed her when she had claimed that she was going to see her mother, but it wasn't just that. Somehow, these days, their friendship just wasn't the same, and she knew who to blame. How dared Kyle take it upon himself to discuss her with *her* friends? And what exactly was it that he had said to them about her?

Fiercely she swallowed back her threatening tears and picked up the phone to ring her mother, leaving a message on the answering machine when there was no response.

Normally, she would have thoroughly enjoyed the opportunity to relax at one of Sally's barbecues and would have gone early to help her friend with the preparations, but now, thanks to Kyle, even that small pleasure was denied her. There was *no* aspect of her life that he hadn't somehow managed to invade, damage even, it seemed, to the extent of turning Sally, her oldest and closest friend, against her. Well, he hadn't vanquished her yet. She had promised him war, and war was exactly what he was going to get, Star decided, gritting her teeth. Beginning with her campaign...

So Kyle thought her work was sexist, did he? Well,

perhaps she could find another way of getting her point across—something he would find easier to relate to…something he would find easier to understand.

Her mind buzzing, fuelled by adrenalin and the challenge of getting the better of him, Star started to work.

Three hours later, her arm stiff from the speed with which she had been working, she finally sat back and studied what she had done, her mouth quirking in a surprisingly youthful and wicked grin.

The first drawing was very similar to the first part of the story-board she had submitted for approval—a factory setting with the workers wilting listlessly in the heat. He was followed by a second drawing showing the same workers looking refreshed and working energetically after the installation of Brad's firm's air-conditioning system. Both scenes were being observed by a *Playboy*-type model.

However, the next pair of drawings bore no resemblance to those she had submitted for the campaign and were strictly for private viewing, Star acknowledged as she surveyed them in triumph; the first of the pair featured the same *Playboy*-type female, partnered in bed by a man whose features were a caricature of Kyle's—and even caricatured he managed to look unexpectedly attractive, Star noted with a frown as she wondered why her attempts to make his chin look weaker and his eyes less magnetic had not worked. He was lying on his back on the rumpled bed, his glance piously averted from his flaccid penis, whilst his partner told him happily that she knew exactly how to put things right.

The next drawing showed the pair of them in an extremely compromising position in the now deserted factory. The newly installed air-conditioning unit was blasting out cold air, but instead of smiling in triumph Kyle's pneumatic lady-friend was eyeing his still unresponsive body dolefully, whilst underneath Star had pencilled in the caption, There are some overheated situations which even we cannot cool down.

What she had done was, Star knew, totally outrageous and would, of course, have to be destroyed. But, even so, it had been worth her aching wrist and the three hours that she had spent working on it just for the satisfaction the result had given her.

Ridiculing Kyle had helped her to get back her sense of perspective.

She still didn't agree with his criticisms of her campaign, but at least now she felt able to reflect on them in a more detached manner, her mind already examining various ways in which she could tone down the elements of the campaign that he had objected to whilst still keeping its essence. She was still convinced that the campaign would work, that its tongue in cheek humour would appeal to potential customers.

It was gone six o'clock. She hadn't had anything to eat since breakfast and she had virtually no food in the flat either. Fortunately, the local supermarket didn't close until eight.

An hour later, as she drove home, her shopping complete, her mood was still triumphantly buoyant. Perhaps she could attend Sally's barbecue after all, she decided— if only to prove to Kyle that *she* wasn't going to let *him* come between her and her friend.

She had just parked her car outside the block of flats and retrieved her shopping from the boot when she was hailed by one of her neighbours.

Amy Stevens was a widow in her early sixties, a small, vague sort of woman who always set Star's teeth slightly on edge, although she berated herself for being so unresponsive to the other woman's obvious attempts to be friendly, telling herself that it wasn't Amy's fault that she came across as being so irritatingly helpless and dependent and that she ought to be more sympathetic towards her loneliness.

'I've just been talking to your new neighbour,' she told Star now. 'Such a charming man. So polite and well mannered. He's an American.'

An American!

Star listened in foreboding as she looked from Amy's face to the blank window of the second-floor flat next to her own.

'He said he'd be staying for several months,' Amy confided, and then added, 'I told him how concerned I was about the fact that just about anyone can drive through the gates into our grounds and he agreed with me that we really ought to have proper security gates fitted.'

Star sighed. The installation of electronic security gates was one of Amy's hobby-horses. Her box of groceries was beginning to make her arms ache, so she used them as an excuse to escape.

She had almost reached the top of the stairs when she heard a door opening onto the landing, followed by the sound of decisive male footsteps crossing the marble floor.

She reached the top of the steps just as he started to descend them and for once she was grateful for Amy's need to chatter as she and Kyle came face to face.

His surprised, 'Star, what are you doing here?' as he automatically reached forward and took hold of her grocery box before she could protest caused her to bare her teeth.

She returned, '*I* live here, as if you didn't know...'

'No, actually I didn't,' he told her curtly, frowning. 'If I had... Which is your flat?' he asked her, glancing round the small hallway with its four doors.

'This one,' Star told him grimly, indicating the door closest to his own.

She already had her key in her hand and as she stepped past him and unlocked her door she held out her arms for her groceries, but to her anger he ignored her, simply stepping past her and into her flat, announcing, 'I'll take these through into the kitchen for you.'

'No, thanks...' Star began, but he was already moving down the narrow hallway, leaving her with no option other than to follow him. She saw him pause as he passed the open door to her sitting room, openly appraising his surroundings.

Star had redecorated the whole flat the year before, choosing colours and fabrics which she felt most at home with—crisp, natural, crunchy linens, smooth, sensuous silks, clean cottons and soft wools, all in harmonising shades of cream and beige, her favourite colours.

Even Lindsay had been surprised the first time Star had allowed her to see all over the flat, marvelling slightly enviously at Star's gift for blending colours and fabrics.

'It's perfect!' she had exclaimed. 'But it just seems so...so unlike you...'

'What did you expect?' Star had asked her wryly as she'd watched Lindsay smoothing down the padded toile cover on her bed. 'A screaming mixture of clashing, angry colours?'

'No, of course not,' Lindsay had denied, but as her friend had studied the small pattern on the cream wallpaper that picked out the soft, muted dark red of the toile bedcover Star had seen that she was completely thrown by Star's choice of decor and Star hadn't felt it necessary to admit to her that her home, these colours, this soothing blend of fabrics and shades were, in fact, a reflection of that part of herself that she preferred to keep most private—that part of herself that was vulnerable and in need sometimes of the calm, soothing comfort of surroundings that provided her with the harmony and almost physical sensual comfort that she had missed as a child.

Sometimes, just to touch her fabrics, to feel their differing strengths and textures beneath her fingertips, to know that they all sprang from natural sources, was enough to soothe even her most turbulent thoughts and memories.

Normally, when she was expecting clients, she closed all the doors to her private rooms, and on their arrival ushered them straight into her work room, and now, as she watched Kyle studying her home, her defences immediately sprang into action so that when he turned to her and asked her quietly, 'Did you choose all this yourself?' she immediately lied.

'No... I have a friend...a client who's an interior designer. She did it.'

Why, when his immediate acceptance of her lie was exactly what she wanted, did she feel such an acute stab of unexpected chagrin at that acceptance?

'You can give those to me now,' she told him curtly, but she had forgotten that the door to her work room was open and that by moving she was almost deliberately inviting Kyle to look towards it and see the drawings that she had left on display.

She tried to close the door, but it was too late. He had already seen what she had done and was moving closer to inspect it more thoroughly.

Star held her breath as she watched him slowly examining all four drawings.

'You've got a good eye for caricature,' was all he said when he had finished. 'But not, it seems, for proportion.'

Proportion?

Star frowned, not understanding until he reached out and indicated her character's flaccid penis.

'I'm just an average-sized guy,' he told her lightly. 'I take a regular size ten or eleven shoe, that's all. I'm no superman!'

To her chagrin Star could feel herself starting to blush as she realised what he meant. If her male character was rather more than averagely well endowed, then she had not made him so on purpose, and, in fact, hadn't been aware of it until he'd pointed it out. A Freudian slip, some might say.

'And she certainly isn't my type,' he added. 'What made you choose her?'

'She's the complete opposite of me,' Star responded angrily before she could stop herself.

'Meaning?' he queried quietly, dangerously focusing on her, refusing to allow her to withdraw her gaze from his.

'I know exactly why you rejected my proposals for the advertising campaign, Kyle, and it has nothing to do with them being sexist,' Star told him angrily.

He was still watching her and for no reason she could name Star felt an odd thrill of high tension course hotly through her body.

'You and I are never going to be able to work together,' she cried out, frustrated by her failure to break free of his penetrating gaze. 'Your male pride, your shallow male ego will never allow you to forget that I showed you to be sexually incompetent.'

As she hurled the insult at him Star had the same sensation in the pit of her stomach as though she had stepped into a lift which had descended too fast, the shock of hearing her own words, of knowing how uncharacteristically out of control she was getting making her feel sick and weak, appalled by what she had said and by the frightening surge of her temper.

It was so unlike her; she was normally so calm and controlled, so logical and coolly incisive in everything she said and did, despite the colour of her hair. Losing one's temper was a sign of weakness, a sign of vulnerability, an admission of self-doubt; she knew that and yet it was too late now to step back from the precipice she herself had so dangerously created. Her pride left her with no other course than to take a deep breath and fling herself over it as she heard Kyle saying with ominous calm, 'Is that a fact? Well, for your information—'

'Whatever you want to say, I don't want to hear,' she cut him off. 'What exactly is it you're trying to prove, Kyle? You come over here…you move into my apartment block…you talk about me…criticise me to my friends, telling them—'

'Oh, no, I'm not letting you get away with that one,' Kyle interrupted her grimly. 'For starters, I'd already agreed to help Brad out over here long before I ever knew you existed, and as for me renting an apartment… It just so happens that the one I'd originally rented fell through—the owners decided not to go abroad as they'd planned, after all—and this was the only suitable vacancy the agents had on their books. If I'd known that you lived here—' He broke off and then told her acidly, 'Get a life, Star. Stop using your past and your father as a stick to beat the rest of the male sex with and an excuse for your emotional immaturity.'

'What emotional immaturity?' Star exploded, her self-control finally giving way beneath the combined pressure of Kyle's unexpectedly skilful attack and her own shock.

'Do I really need to tell you? You're the one who said that the only kind of intimacy you wanted to share with a man was a sexual one, that you were too afraid of the potential pain any kind of emotional intimacy might cause to risk—'

'I *never* said that,' Star interrupted him furiously.

'Not in so many words,' Kyle agreed with a shrug. 'But it's obvious that you *are* afraid—'

'No. That isn't true,' Star denied vehemently, shaking her head. 'It isn't true. And I don't… You can't… I want you to leave,' she managed to calm down enough to tell him shakily as she tried to control the way her body was starting to tremble inwardly as well as outwardly.

She started to turn her back on him, terrified of him

seeing how traumatically his quietly voiced words had
affected her, but before she could he reached out and
took hold of her wrist, the expression in his eyes suddenly changing as his thumb registered the too fast, nervous race of her pulse.

Her strangled, 'Let go of me,' was ignored as he insisted,

'Look at me, Star! Look at me!'

She wanted to refuse, but somehow she could not do
so, her gaze lifting angrily and defiantly to meet his as
she tensed her muscles against his mental invasion of
her emotions in much the same way as a nervous young
virgin might have tensed her body against a more physical intrusion.

'I'm right, aren't I?' he challenged her softly. 'You
are afraid of committing yourself emotionally to a
man…to a relationship…'

'Go to hell,' Star hurled inelegantly at him as she
finally managed to pull her wrist free. 'And get out of
my flat…'

To her relief he began to walk back towards the front
door, but before he got there he paused, then turned
round and simply looked at her, subjecting her whole
body—from the tips of her toes to the top of her head—
to a slow, seeking inspection of such unexpected and
open sensuality that Star actually felt herself starting to
curl her toes—an instinctive feminine reaction to the effect he was having on her.

She had been appraised sexually by men before,
many, many times, but she had never experienced anything like this. It was like comparing… It was like comparing sex to making love, she acknowledged unwillingly as she heard Kyle saying softly to her, 'And for
your information, Star, I didn't walk away from you that
night because I didn't want you, but because I did. Just
like I do right now. *Just* like I do right now… Oh, yes,'
he continued, when he heard her indrawn breath, 'right

now there is nothing…nothing that the most primitive,
basic male part of me wants more than to pick you up
and carry you into your bedroom and lay your beautiful,
naked body beneath mine whilst I prove to you just how
very, very wrong you are…'

'Really?' Suddenly Star was back on safer, familiar
ground, her voice gaining strength and developing a cynically mocking undertone as she challenged him, 'So
what's stopping you? Surely not the fear that you don't
compare well with my…drawing?'

Star slid him a tantalising, slant-eyed look of laughing
invitation but instead of taking her up on it Kyle shook
his head and told her gently, 'No! *You* are…or rather
your fear, your refusal to let yourself let go of the past
and to stop punishing yourself for your father's faults.
You aren't to blame because he wasn't there for you,
Star. *He* is, and when the day finally comes when you
can accept that, when you can share real intimacy with
me instead of wanting to use sex as a means of punishing
me for being a man, then—'

'Don't hold your breath,' Star advised him bitingly.
Did he really think that she was stupid enough to believe
in what he was saying?

When she could share real *intimacy*… Any woman
who thought that she could do that with a man had to
be a fool. It was like opening your door and inviting a
thief to walk in and help himself.

As Kyle closed her front door behind him, Star's telephone started to ring. She went to answer it, frowning
as she heard her mother's voice, her frown deepening as
her mother explained that Star could not visit her over
the weekend as she was going away with a 'friend'.

Her mother's coy use of the word made Star grimly
demand to know just who her 'friend' was, but her
mother, characteristically, refused to answer her.

Another man, Star guessed, but refrained from saying
so.

Well, there was no way she was going to change her mind and go to Sally's barbecue now, she decided when she hung up. She would just have to pretend that she was still going to her mother's; after all, it wasn't as though she didn't have plenty of work to occupy her, she acknowledged as she glanced towards the drawings which had caused her such amusement and release earlier.

Now that the adrenalin buzz of excitement had drained away, leaving her feeling irritated with herself and deflated, she viewed the sketches in a different light, grimacing in distaste as she removed them and ripped them up. It had been a childish thing to do and something which she was now uncomfortably aware had, in a way, backfired on her and degraded her more than it had Kyle.

What it had also done, though, was give her several ideas on how she could subtly alter her original campaign. Quickly she retrieved her box of groceries and took them into the kitchen. Food first and then work, she promised herself.

And that was another advantage of working from home. There were no problems about working late into the night, nor did she have to get up early in the morning to get to an office. She could work all night and then drop into bed with the dawn if she wanted—and indeed had done so on occasion.

As she unpacked her groceries, she tried not to think about the fact that Kyle was now living right next door, his bedroom separated from hers by only a single internal wall.

His bedroom… Now why the hell should she be thinking about that…? Angrily she slammed the fridge door closed. There was no reason, none at all. She didn't want him…she just wanted to prove to herself that she was right… Not that she had any doubts on that score, she assured herself hastily. Of course she didn't. How could she have? No, of course she didn't... It was just...

Star cursed as she realised that she was trying to open a carton of milk from the wrong side, and urged herself to concentrate on what she was doing, as milk spilled from the carton and down over her wrist onto the worktop.

CHAPTER SIX

STAR glowered ferociously at the sun shining through her kitchen window. The sky was a soft haze of blue and already, at just gone eight in the morning, she could feel the heat in the sun—a perfect day for a barbecue. Except that *she* wouldn't be going to it; *she* would not in fact be going anywhere, thanks to Kyle and, of course, her mother.

She could see the postman walking towards the apartment block; the contract gardeners employed to keep their small grounds neat and weed-free were already at work, the boxes of bedding plants that they were removing from their truck reminding Star that her own small balcony area and window-boxes needed attention. That at least was something she could do with her day in addition to working.

She heard her letter box rattle as the post arrived and padded barefoot into her hall to collect it, her body stiffening as she recognised her father's handwriting on a large square envelope that looked suspiciously as if it contained some kind of formal invitation. Not another wedding, she decided sardonically; surely even he had grown tired now of constantly changing partners?

It *was* a wedding invitation, Star discovered, but for her stepsister's wedding rather than her father's.

Emily was not one of her father's other children but the eldest daughter of his second wife. Even after he and her mother had divorced, and despite the fact that she was not his natural child, Emily had stayed close to

Star's father—much closer than she had done herself, Star acknowledged as she remembered her old childhood bitterness and resentment over the closeness that her father and Emily had shared.

Star could still remember the pain and resentment she had suffered on her rare visits to her father, when she had seen how differently he'd treated Emily from the way he'd treated her. She remembered how shut out and unwanted she had felt and how much it had hurt knowing that he loved Emily more than he loved her... Hurt... She frowned.

Now it seemed that the bond between Emily and her father was as close as ever since he was obviously hosting the wedding and giving Emily away.

Typically of her father, the invitation included a brief, handwritten instruction that she was to stay for the weekend and that he would book rooms for her and a friend, if she cared to bring one, at a local hotel. He explained:

> Unfortunately we cannot put you up at the house as Emily will be staying, of course, along with her fiancé, and of course the twins will be down from university and both of them want to bring their current partner with them. So I know you'll understand...

Her father possessed a magnificent seven bedroom Georgian rectory which he had bought for next to nothing early in the eighties but Star could well understand that with so many children of his own, plus steps, there would indeed be no room for her. When had there ever been?

She remembered vividly how, on her first ever visit to him, he had had to go out and buy her a sleeping bag and she had had to suffer the indignity of sleeping on the floor of the landing of the small house he had been sharing with Emily's mother. Emily, of course, had had her own room but Star had been barred from sharing it because apparently she'd frightened Emily.

She flung the invitation down on the kitchen table. She wasn't going to go; why should she? Why should she once again be made to feel the outsider, the unwanted interloper? Let Emily play the adored and adoring stepdaughter if she wished, but she was going to play it without her as an audience, Star decided grimly.

Suddenly the brightness of the sunshine irritated her and she yanked down the blind over the kitchen window, blotting it out.

She could well imagine what would be said about her in her absence when she did not turn up for Emily's wedding, but *she* didn't care, she told herself bitterly. Why should she? When had any of *them*, but more especially her father, cared about her?

After she had finished her breakfast coffee she reminded herself that she was supposed to be visiting her mother—the excuse that she had given Sally for not attending her barbecue—and that the last thing she needed was for Sally to find out that she hadn't gone away at all. With Kyle living next door, even if she hadn't seen anything more of him since their altercation, it was more than likely that Sally would learn that she had lied about her mother if she stayed in her flat.

Reminding herself that she needed plants, compost and several other bits and pieces if she was going to spend the late afternoon and early evening working on her baskets and tubs, she decided that rather than purchase them from a local garden centre she might as well take the opportunity to visit a very highly acclaimed centre which specialised in the more unusual plants and which was a good hour's drive away.

It was early evening when Star finally returned home. A quick search around the car park confirmed that there was—as she had expected—no sign of Kyle's four-wheel drive.

As she unloaded her car she tried not to think about how unsettling her day had been. The fine weather had brought out a good many visitors to the garden centre, families in the main—tight-knit, self-contained, exclusive units of mother, father and offspring.

Fathers had changed since her childhood; now they were far more involved with their children, far more physically affectionate with them. Seeing them today with their children had brought back the pain and misery of her own fatherless childhood—emotions exacerbated, she had no doubt, by the receipt of her father's note this morning. Despite what Kyle seemed to think, she did not need a counsellor—or anyone else—to explain her own emotions to her; she understood them all too well.

By now Sally and Chris's barbecue would be in full swing, their small garden filled with their mutual friends. They were a good crowd, sociable and entertaining, with a wide variety of interests and a very cosmopolitan outlook on life, and Star knew that she would have enjoyed being there with them. But, thanks to Kyle, she could not be.

No doubt right now he would be charming all the women whilst still managing to earn the respect of the men; she had seen how highly Brad thought of him. And no doubt Sally would have managed to introduce Lindsay to him by now. And Sally was quite right, of course—Lindsay *was* exactly his type.

Would he look deep into Lindsay's eyes and tell her that for him sex without emotion was like a flower without perfume? If he did Star could well imagine the effect it would have on her far too vulnerable friend. And when he drove Lindsay home and she asked him in for a cup of coffee would he hold her and kiss her and then tell her—?

Stop it, Star warned herself angrily as she carried her plants up to her flat. Why should *she* care *what* he said to Lindsay or how her friend reacted? She cared because Lindsay *was* her friend, she told herself defensively. That was all... Her thoughts, her feelings were nothing to do with her emotions. The anger and bitterness that she could feel coiling so tightly in her chest were on Lindsay's behalf, not her own.

It took several journeys to carry all her purchases up to her flat and once that was done she opened the French windows onto her private balcony area and started to remove her display of pansies, whispering tenderly to them that they would be quite safe and that they would enjoy their new home in a protected corner of the flats' grounds which she had earmarked for them.

Once this had been done it was already past eight o'clock and beginning to grow slightly dusk, though the air was still warm. Star worked on. What, after all, was the point of stopping? What else had she to do other than to compose a note declining her father's invitation to Emily's wedding?

The pots were now complete. She had decided on a scheme of all white flowers this time, having seen a similar display in the corner of the garden centre. White... How bridal... Emily would be thrilled, she taunted herself, but in some countries wasn't white also the colour of mourning?

Mourning... Star sat back on her heels and closed her eyes. What the hell had she to mourn? Nothing, thanks to her wisdom in making sure she did not fall into the same trap as the rest of her sex and allow a man to steal her heart and then destroy her life.

At eleven o'clock she tucked the final plant into place. The balcony needed cleaning where she had spilled compost on it but she would leave that until morning, she decided tiredly as she opened the door slightly to allow some air into the sitting room whilst she stripped off her grimy clothes and showered.

Kyle frowned as he drew up outside the block of flats and saw the lights on in Star's flat. According to Sally, she was supposed to be away for the weekend.

His frown deepened as he got out of his car and realised that Star's balcony door was open. It would be an easy enough task for a burglar to climb up to it and break in; the locks were flimsy enough, as he had seen from his own, and Amy had told him only the previous morning that she was concerned about the lack of security.

He was just wondering what he ought to do when he saw Star's car. What was she doing at home? Had she, perhaps, come back unexpectedly and surprised an intruder? If so...

Kyle took the stairs two at a time, then rapped firmly on Star's door. Star heard it as she came out of the shower. Frowning, she pulled the belt of her robe a little more securely around her waist and went to the door. Chances were that it would only be one of her neighbours—Amy, more than likely, unable to sleep and come for a chat.

Her hair, wet from her shower, was wrapped in a towel turban-style on top of her head, and with her face free from make-up she looked, although she didn't know it, more like the solemn child she had been than the woman she now was.

As she opened the door the last person she was expecting to see was Kyle. He at least, so far as her imagination was concerned, was very cosily ensconced in Lindsay's home, no doubt offering her solace and comfort of a kind that made Star's upper lip curl in disdain just to think about it.

Only he wasn't. He was standing outside her front door. In her hall now, in fact, she recognised as he closed the door firmly and demanded tersely, 'Are you all right?'

'Yes, of course I'm all right. Why shouldn't I be?' she challenged him.

'Sally said you were going to spend the weekend with your mother. When I drove up and saw your lights on and the balcony door open, I thought you might have had burglars—'

'And so you knocked on my door, hoping that they would let you in,' she scoffed. 'Is that what you are trying to tell me?'

'No. I knew you must be here because I saw your car, but I thought...' He paused, raking his fingers through his hair, all too aware of how she was likely to react if he told her what had been running through his mind. A woman on her own...vulnerable...beautiful...and with the kind of temperament all too likely to push a couple of thugs into...

'What are you doing here, anyway?' he demanded instead. 'Sally told me that your mother lives down on the south coast.'

'Yes, she does,' Star agreed uncommunicatively. It was unfortunate that he knew that she hadn't been away but she would just explain to Sally what had happened, only changing the timing so that she could pretend that she hadn't realised her mother would be away until it was too late to change her mind about the barbecue, and, after all, so far as Kyle went she owed him no explanations. None at all.

'I was just about to go to bed—' she began, and then stopped as she saw it—the tell-tale mark of another woman's lipstick on his jaw... Lipstick on his jaw and... Her nostrils quivered fastidiously as she moved slightly closer to him and caught the scent of perfume on his clothes—Lindsay's perfume; she would have recognised it anywhere.

A sudden sense of fate having played into her hands, having dealt her all the cards she needed to win, made her feel almost dizzily reckless. Now was her chance to prove what she already knew. He had come here to her flat straight from another woman...from her friend with whom he had been sharing—if she was any judge, and she was—an intimate goodnight... A very intimate goodnight, she decided bitterly as she saw another lipstick stain, this time close to his ear.

Much as it went against the grain, the time had come for her to use a little subtle subterfuge. This was, after all, war, she reminded herself as she lowered both her voice and her eyes and murmured mock-dulcetly, 'It was kind of you to come and check that I was all right.' A contrite smile curled her mouth. 'I was just about to have some supper; would you like to join me or did you have enough at the barbecue?'

For a moment Star thought that he might have cottoned onto the secret meaning underlying her words. He certainly looked rather sharply at her but as she held her breath and waited he simply said, 'A cup of coffee would be very welcome.'

'A cup of coffee... Well, I think I can manage that.'

The balcony windows were still open and as she went to close them Star deliberately shook her damp hair free of its constraining towel; her cotton robe was only thin and with any luck the light from behind her ought to give him a pretty clear impression of exactly what it was concealing.

Star knew without vanity that she had a very sensual body—strong-boned and yet at the same time alluringly, femininely curved and delicate, her waist narrow, her hips softly curved, whilst her breasts were taut and firm, her nipples, now that she was standing in the cooling night air, suddenly stiff. A little too much so, she decided as she turned away from the window and made her way to the kitchen... It never did to overgild the lily, and in her experience men preferred to believe that only they could have *that* particular effect on a woman.

Male egos—how much damage they caused...how much pain and misery. If he responded to her sexual overtures now, it would prove beyond any shadow of a doubt—not that she had any doubts— that she *was* right about him, that beneath that assumed demeanour of caring sensitivity he was just as self-centred and untrustworthy as the rest of his sex, and that his claim to want to make an emotional commitment to a woman was just another male ploy designed to trick a woman into trusting him.

If he was genuinely even one tenth of the man he claimed to be, there was no way he would be able to respond to her overtures having just, quite obviously, made love with Lindsay. But of course he wasn't what he claimed to be at all; she knew that.

She walked into the kitchen, her body movements deliberately subtle and sensually enticing, and Star knew that he was watching her as he followed her into the small, confined space. As she filled the kettle she smiled at him and purred, 'Why don't you make yourself comfortable?'

He didn't look at her as he sat down but Star knew that he had to be conscious of the firm yet seductively soft curves of her breasts, which were now virtually on a level with his eyes. There wasn't an awful lot of room in her small kitchen, but there was no real need for him to move his outstretched legs so betrayingly, turning away from her slightly as he removed his jacket and placed it over his thighs.

The invitation from her father was still on the table

and as she carried his coffee over to him she picked it up quickly.

'A duty invitation from my father—a way of underlining the fact that Emily is so much more the kind of daughter he prefers, all pliable sweetness and wanting to please...'

'Emily?' Kyle was frowning, Star saw, and she wished that she had not made any reference to the letter and wondered why on earth she had.

'Your half-sister?' he quizzed in that open, interested way that Americans seemed to have.

'No,' Star snapped grittily. 'She's my stepsister. Louise, her mother, was my father's second wife; they're divorced now but Emily has always stayed in contact with my father. She claims she looks on him as her real father. God knows why, since he and Louise were only together for four years before he ditched her for a new, younger model—just long enough for her to produce the twins and for him to get bored.

'After Louise came Harriet—no previous convictions—sorry, children. That lasted five years and produced Anne and Sam and then...let me think...Gemma or Jemima. I can't quite remember.

'You see, by then the visits had trickled down to one or two a year. There wasn't any room, you see...not with all those children who needed a father so much more than I did... And, of course, I was such a difficult child, so disruptive with the little ones, not like Emily who was always so sweet and loving with them. They all adored her...all the wives...but they were all so alike...and all the best of friends... Tragic, really, in a black-comedy sort of fashion.

'And now it's Lucinda's turn. She and Emily are close friends. In fact I seem to remember being told that they were at school together, although I suspect that Emily might have been in a higher class. She's only three years older than me, you see, and Dad's taste runs to sweet, innocent young things.

'He must be getting rather tired now, I imagine, because they've been together three years, but then, of course, the triplets are very energetic—not easy for a man in his late fifties, although he does try not to show it.

'No doubt he'll fully enjoy the role of father of the bride, although Emily will have to make sure that she always believes that *he's* the most important man in her life, and he won't like it when she makes him a grandfather—'

'So you're not going to the wedding, then?' Kyle interrupted her quietly.

'Weddings aren't my style,' Star told him curtly, and added vehemently, 'No, I won't be going—not that I'll be missed. It's only a duty invite. No doubt someone, probably Emily, has even had to remind him that I exist.

'The truth is that my father would like to believe that I don't exist. I'm not his kind of daughter, you see... I'm not the kind he can show off to his friends as his pretty, adoring little girl. Emily's much more suited to fulfilling that role than me.

'And then, of course, if I did go, there'd be the usual comments that I'm not fulfilling my traditional female role, that I'm not decorating the arm of some suitably impressive man—but not as impressive as my father, of course.'

Star suddenly realised that not only had she raised her voice above its normal level, cool pitch, but also that, shamingly, it was filled with angry emotion. What on earth was wrong with her? What had possessed her to reveal so much about herself—to *betray* so much about herself?

As Kyle watched the emotions chase one another across her face—anger, confusion, dismay, disbelief and, most telling of all, pain—he wanted to reach out to her, to take hold of her and make her whole again, heal all her hurts, show her that she was wrong, that she was perfect and fully worthy of being loved just as she was. *Just* as she was. And he also knew exactly how she would react if he tried, if he let her see how vulnerable he knew she was beneath that shield of prickly pride and acid cynicism that she used to protect herself.

He could see her so clearly as the child she must have been—an outsider…different…sensitive, and far too intelligent not to be aware of the prejudices and flaws in the adults around her.

'I could come with you to the wedding if you like,' he said.

The offer stopped Star dead in her tracks. She was already furiously angry with herself and thoroughly bewildered by her uncharacteristic behaviour, and Kyle's words had left her totally nonplussed and bereft of her normal ability to make a quick, defensive comeback—unable to do anything other than simply demand huskily, 'Why?'

Kyle had no intention of telling her why; instead he simply shrugged and answered, 'Why not?'

'I'm not going; there isn't any point,' Star said fiercely.

'Yes, there is,' Kyle contradicted her. 'He is your father; they are all your family—'

'I don't *have* a father,' Star told him flatly. 'Nor a family; and I don't want one either. I'm not going.'

'Just like you didn't go to Sally's barbecue tonight. Funny,' Kyle told her with deceptive gentleness, 'I hadn't thought of *you* as the type to run away from a situation that made you feel vulnerable. It just goes to show—'

'I did not run away,' Star interrupted him angrily. 'And nothing, no one makes me feel vulnerable.'

Her eyes warned him against continuing but Kyle ignored the fiercely challenging look she was giving him, telling her, 'If you really believe that, then you are lying, Star, and not just to me but, more importantly, to yourself, pretending—'

'Pretending!' Star had had enough. 'I'm not the one who's pretending,' she stormed at him. 'You're...'

To her horror Star suddenly found that she couldn't go on—that her throat was closing up, her eyes filling with tears. Tears... She never cried. Ever.

As Kyle saw first the disbelief and then the panic crossing her face as her eyes filled with tears and her throat muscles constricted, he decided that there was a time in every man's life when he could allow himself to stop listening to his inner voice of caution and act on his instincts instead.

Through the blur of her tears, Star saw him stand up and come towards her but didn't realise what he was going to do until she felt his arms come round her, holding her, drawing her firmly against his body, one hand securing her against him whilst the other rubbed her back in the same comforting way that she had seen parents comforting small children.

For some reason what he was doing, instead of restoring her to sanity, seemed to have the perverse effect of making her cry harder, in deep, gulping sobs accompanied by ridiculously childish hiccups, whilst his voice murmured soft words of comfort in her ear.

Men did not treat her like this, cuddling her and comforting her as though she were a small child; she did not behave like this—crying, clinging, wanting to be held, to feel secure...comforted...understood.

Understood. She stopped crying, her body tensing in rejection of Kyle's hold on it as she started to pull away.

Kyle, who until that moment had managed to make his body understand that on this occasion she was not a

highly desirable and sensual woman but a very unhappy
and needy child, was very quickly reminded by that
same body that those deliciously warm and feminine
breasts that he could feel and virtually see beneath her
thin covering did not belong to any child. He warned
himself of all the reasons there were for not allowing
himself to feel what he was feeling right now and then
promptly ignored them as Star lifted her face up to his,
her lips parting, ready to deliver what he knew would
be some scathing and furious criticism of his behaviour.

What was it about the combination of vulnerability
and strength in a woman's face when it was wet with
tears at the same time as her eyes were full of fury that
evoked such an instant and age old male response? he
wondered helplessly as he looked from her angry eyes
to her softly parted mouth and gave up the struggle to
resist the temptation in front of him.

Kyle kissed her, the unexpectedness of the warm pressure of his mouth on hers causing her eyes to widen in
shock as she stared up at him in disbelief, her body motionless in his arms, as caught off guard as a young,
untried girl.

She tasted wonderful, Kyle acknowledged, her mouth
as sharply sweet as a delicious piece of fruit, tormenting
his taste buds, making him want to take more and more.

Star blinked dizzily as he lifted his mouth from hers,
touching her lips with the tip of his tongue. She looked
at Kyle's mouth and then raised her gaze to his eyes,
her own cloudy and confused. An involuntary shudder
went through her body; she looked back at Kyle's
mouth.

That look wasn't faked or contrived, Kyle knew; he
doubted that she even knew what she was doing or the
effect it was having on him, he didn't have to hear her
whisper huskily, 'Kiss me,' to know what she wanted
and she didn't have to ask him for it either. He was

covering her mouth with his own even before she had
finished saying it, kissing the way he'd wanted to kiss
her right from the very start.

Star had ceased to exist on her normal plane from the
moment she had discovered that she was going to cry.
Now she was vaguely aware of somehow, somewhere
along the line, stepping out of her normal persona, her
normal behaviour, but it hardly seemed worth concern-
ing herself about when the movement of Kyle's mouth
on her own was filling her with the kind of physical
sensation that would have made the explosion that led
to the creation of the universe a mere nothing.

When her head fell back against Kyle's supporting
arm to allow his mouth easy access to the taut line of
her throat, she whimpered in fierce, excited pleasure,
digging her nails into the strong muscles of his back and
raking it passionately as she shivered beneath his caress,
her breasts lifting, their nipples taut and dark and clearly
visible beneath their thin covering.

She was kissing him too, hungry, biting kisses inter-
spersed with the shallow, frantic sound of her breathing,
making Kyle want to wrench the thin covering off her
body and slide his hand between those long, slender legs
to find out if her womanhood had that same delicious,
succulent moistness as her mouth.

He wanted to touch her with his fingers and to carry
the scent and taste of her to his lips, to lick the flavour
of her from them and then kiss her whilst he still had
the taste of her in his mouth, to make her know that
once the immediacy of their shared desire to come together was sated he wanted to repeat that intimacy by
replacing his fingers with his mouth—and if there was
any possibility that she might share his desire and sim-
ilarly want to explore and know him, then…

Star whimpered deep in her throat as she felt the puls-
ing ache inside her body grow to a heated throb. She

couldn't wait much longer. She had never wanted a man with such...such intensity, such overwhelming insistence.

Her hands moved down over Kyle's body, his mouth silencing her small purr of satisfaction with a kiss of fierce male hunger as she felt the hard surge of his erection. She didn't want him like this, quickly and frantically, the pleasure gone almost before she could enjoy it. She wanted...she wanted...

Dragging her mouth from his, she told him huskily, 'Not here... In bed... I want...I want you in bed, Kyle... All of you, not just...'

He seemed to understand without her having to say any more because he was already turning towards the door, letting her guide him to where she wanted him to be, taking control only when she opened the bedroom door, pulling her back into his arms and kissing her deeply, using his tongue to show her the pleasure his body would soon be giving her, giving them *both*, as he pushed her robe off her shoulders and explored her body blindly with a delicate fingertip touch that left her shuddering and clinging achingly to him.

However, when she reached towards him and tried to undress him, he pushed her gently away and told her softly, 'No, not yet... I want to look at you...see you...know you first, Star.'

She had no inhibitions about her body and felt no shame about her sexuality or her needs, and yet for the first time in her life, as he took a step back from her and silently, lingeringly let his gaze rove over her body, she knew what it was to experience uncertainty and insecurity—so much so that she actually found that she was holding her breath, wondering, worrying that... And then she looked into his eyes and her pent-up fear leaked away on an unsteady lurch of sharp emotion.

'Star...' She could hear in the husky, shaken timbre

of his voice all that she wanted to know—his awe, his desire, his adoration of the perfect femaleness of her.

Her confidence returning, she waited for him to come to her, to take her in his arms, and he kissed her slowly and lingeringly as he picked her up and carried her towards the bed. By the time he reached it his mouth had travelled as far as the tiny hollow at the base of her throat. By the time he lowered her onto it he was caressing the smooth slope of her breast. By the time she was actually lying on it his mouth had reached the rigid peak of her nipple, and she expelled a long, slow moan of satisfaction as his gentle caress became firmer, stronger, his kiss turning to a rhythmic suckle. Blindly Star reached for him, her hands tugging at his shirt, and then she smelt it…that unmistakable scent of another woman's perfume.

It was like free falling without the security of a parachute, knowing that only pain lay ahead, that there was no escape from it. No hope of any safety. And with her knowledge of that pain came shock, anger and panic.

There was no need for her to do any more. She had all the proof she needed. She had been so right to mistrust him. These and a hundred other thoughts she didn't want to acknowledge raced through her brain, her body awash now with confused emotions and sensations.

Valiantly she tried to recover her lost ground, to convince herself that what had happened had all been part of her grand plan, that she had known what she was doing all the time, that she had simply pretended to want him, that she had never really been in any danger of losing control.

As he felt her body stiffen in rejection of his touch, Kyle lifted his head to look at her.

'Thank you,' Star told him, 'but there's no need for you to go any further. You've already proved my point for me…proved that I was right about you…'

'Right about me?' Kyle could see the antipathy glittering in her eyes and hear the contempt in her voice but he had no idea what it was he was supposed to have done.

'You're a fake, Kyle,' Star told him triumphantly. 'A liar...a cheat...no different from the rest of your sex... You didn't want just sex—sex without emotion—remember?'

Kyle closed his eyes and held onto his self-control—just. Now he understood. He knew what was happening, what she was trying to do. Self-preservation, self-protection was all very well and his compassion helped him to accept her need to deny what was happening between them, to reject the emotions that he was pretty damn sure she felt as strongly as he did in favour of the safer alternative of mere physical need, but he was still a man, after all, and right now...

'Star,' he told her firmly, 'there's no way that what we're experiencing...*sharing*...could ever remotely be described as "just sex". I understand that it's difficult for you—'

'No?' Star cut across him bitingly. 'So it wasn't sex; what was it, then? Love?' she challenged him mockingly. The harsh tone of her voice jarred but Kyle refused to allow her to force him into a fight.

'I don't know,' he told her softly. 'But what I *do* know is that there was a hell of a lot more going on between us just then than the mere physical arousal of two bodies—'

'Really? Well, you should know. I suppose you said the same thing to Lindsay, did you?'

'Lindsay?'

He was an actor, Star acknowledged, she had to give him that, but then of course he would have to be able to carry off the kind of act he liked to put on.

'Yes, Lindsay,' she repeated tauntingly. 'Remember

her...? She's the one you were with before me...the one whose lipstick you were still wearing when you came in...the one whose perfume you are still wearing right now. Right here.'

She let her fingertips touch his throat and the open neck of his shirt—the open neck she had further unfastened in her desire to touch him and hold him, to—

The savage, raking pain that tore at her was surely far too intense to be put down to mere anger against men and their perfidy, their deceit... But determinedly she ignored that knowledge and instead tried to find release from it by digging her fingernails into his skin purposefully, painfully before releasing him, her mouth curling in disdain as she told him, 'You smell of her perfume... Of her...'

Those last two words weren't true, but Star didn't care. She wanted him to know how completely he had betrayed himself, how utterly contemptible she found him.

'And just for the record,' she added, determined now to settle every single score, '*I* never really wanted you, Kyle...not even just for sex. You're not my type. All I wanted was to show you how pathetic you are and how easy it is to see through your lies.'

Kyle had had enough. Compassion was one thing; allowing her crazy paranoia to go unchallenged and unchecked was something else again.

'I do not lie,' he told her grimly. 'I don't have the need. Neither do I have the need to create some fantasy world for myself filled with fantasy villains because it's the only way I have of trying to pretend that I haven't been hurt and that I'm not afraid and vulnerable. *I* don't need to cling to the belief that all women are like my mother and that because she didn't want me and she walked out on me that means that I was to blame, that her inability to mother me lies with me. Your father walked out on his marriage and you because—'

'It wasn't my fault... It's not true... I tried to be good, to be what he wanted.'

White-faced, Star almost screamed the words at him as the angry tears flooded her eyes.

'No, Star,' Kyle agreed gently, 'that's right—it wasn't your fault—but deep down inside you don't really believe that, do you? Just as you refuse to believe that you might just possibly be wrong...that I might just possibly have genuinely wanted you, physically and emotionally...that I haven't lied at all, that—'

'Go to hell,' Star screamed at him. 'How can you want me when you've come to me from Lindsay's bed? I don't believe you.'

'No?' Kyle queried thickly, his patience finally snapping. 'Then try believing this...'

Star couldn't believe how quickly he overpowered her, taking hold of her and imprisoning her flailing arms whilst he silenced her furious protests with his mouth, kissing her with an angry passion that excited a response inside her that blasted apart her self-control and had her clinging to him, fighting fire with fire, kissing him back with just as much furious sexual urgency as he was showing her, knowing that it wasn't just the hard pressure of his hold on her that was welding her body to his, knowing that his visible physical arousal only mirrored the inner secret ache of her own.

'I have not been making love to Lindsay... I have never, would never go from one woman's bed, one woman's *body*,' he emphasised, 'to another's.

'I could take things to their natural conclusion between us now—take *you* now,' he told her rawly, 'and prove to you just how wrong you are, not just about me but about yourself. God knows I want to. But if I did I would be breaking one of the rules I've made for myself, which is never to touch a woman in anger. But then you aren't a woman really, are you, Star? You're just a hurt, angry child, wildly hitting out at every man who comes near her because the one man she needs to love her doesn't.'

His mouth smiled as he caught the warning hiss of her indrawn breath but his eyes didn't. His eyes, Star registered painfully, were completely blank of any emotion, and as he released her and got off the bed she started to shiver with reaction.

Her pride wouldn't allow her to conceal her body; instead, she stood up and held her head up proudly, following him to the door. When he reached it, he paused and turned to face her. Was it her imagination or did a tiny muscle beat frantically in his jaw as he looked at her?

'And, for your information, the only woman that I...my *skin*...my *body*...could possibly smell of tonight is you. I wanted to fall asleep with the scent of you all around me. The taste of you in my mouth. Did you know that?' he asked her quietly.

To her shock he suddenly came up to her and bent his head to kiss her naked breast before telling her thickly, 'I wanted to taste you not just here but here as well.' And then, before she could stop him, he touched her briefly but deliberately, intimately, just where her body was still achingly moist and ready for him.

Star couldn't stop herself from betraying her shocked reaction. It burned two bright red spots of colour high on her cheekbones and tightened her already over-taut muscles.

'Yes, I know,' Kyle said heavily to her. 'You want me to go!'

Speechless, Star watched him as he walked into her kitchen and re-emerged carrying his discarded jacket. She waited for what felt like a very long time after he

had gone before walking unsteadily to her door to lock
and secure it.

Nothing in her life, in her experience, had prepared
her, *could* have prepared her for what had just happened... Nothing and no one.

CHAPTER SEVEN

'I'M REALLY sorry you had to miss the barbecue, you would have enjoyed it,' Sally sympathised as she handed Star one of the mugs of coffee that she had just made, settling herself onto one of the pair of garden chairs that she had drawn up on the patio overlooking her garden.

Star had planned to spend the whole day working but a phone call from Sally halfway through the morning, inviting her over for a coffee and a natter, had changed her mind.

'How was your mother?' Sally added solicitously.

She was fine, Star was about to say, but then she shook her head and admitted quietly, 'I never went to see her. She...she... There was a mix-up over the arrangements and—'

'Oh, Star, why on earth didn't you come round?' Sally chastised her.

'I...I wasn't really in the mood... I...I'm having a bit of a problem with this campaign for Brad...and I—'

'But you were so excited about it,' Sally reminded her.

'Yes, I was,' Star agreed, 'but that was before...'

'That was before you realised you'd be working so closely with Kyle?' Sally suggested. 'Oh, Star, I wish you could... I wish the two of you had hit it off better,' she amended tactfully. 'He was a real hit with everyone on Saturday.'

'Really?' Star tried to keep her voice flatly uninterested and non-committal, but she knew that she had failed when she saw Sally frown. Part of her itched to tell Sally the truth about her precious, wonderful Kyle, to tell her how he had come straight to her bed, her arms from Lindsay's, but another part of her—a new, unfamiliar, illogical part of her—shrank from revealing to even so close a friend as Sally just what had happened.

'Mind you, I still haven't managed to find anyone for Kyle,' Sally admitted ruefully. 'I introduced him to Lindsay and the two of them were chatting for simply ages. I even saw Lindsay fling her arms around him and give him a kiss at one point and I thought... She disappeared shortly afterwards but Kyle stayed on, although not for much longer.

'However, Lindsay rang me the day after to tell me that, thanks to the heart-to-heart conversation she'd had with Kyle, she'd realised how much Miles meant to her and how much she wanted to save her marriage and so she had gone straight home and telephoned him to tell him so.

'He apparently had been feeling exactly the same way and the upshot of the whole thing is that they've decided to give their marriage a second chance. She was even talking about them starting a family,' Sally added slightly wistfully.

Kyle had been having a heart-to-heart with Lindsay about her marriage. Kyle had *not* taken Lindsay home... Lindsay had kissed him out of gratitude and happiness. Kyle and Lindsay had *not* been lovers. He had *not* come straight from Lindsay's arms, from her bed to her own.

'Star...what is it? Are you feeling all right?' she heard Sally asking her anxiously.

'Yes, yes, I'm fine,' she assured her friend.

'You look dreadful. I thought you were going to faint, you went so pale,' Sally told her.

'I...I've just been a little tired; this campaign...I've been...'

'Why don't you talk to Kyle about it?' Sally suggested practically. 'Perhaps he could—'

'No.' Star cut her off sharply, firmly changing the subject by asking her, 'Have you managed to change Chris's mind yet about the two of you starting a family?'

It was no secret to Sally's friends that she wanted a baby.

'I'm still working on it,' Sally admitted. 'I know we both agreed that we wanted several years together before we even started thinking about a family, but since both Poppy and Claire have become pregnant... It isn't that Chris doesn't want children; it's just that he feels we're not ready for them yet. I know what he means, but I just feel so...'

'Broody?' Star supplied for her dryly.

'Well, yes,' Sally confessed. 'We're off to Italy at the end of September, Poppy and James are lending us the villa for a month and I'm hoping to work on him then.'

'Perhaps he feels that having a baby is becoming more important to you than he is,' Star suggested.

Sally looked shocked. 'Oh, no...he couldn't think that...could he?'

'You have become rather obsessive about it,' Star pointed out.

'Mmm...a bit like you with this thing you've got about men in general and poor Kyle in particular, do you mean?' Sally came back slyly.

'I've got to go,' Star told her quickly, and finished her coffee. 'I've got a deadline to meet...'

'So have I,' Sally said mischievously. 'I want to be pregnant by Christmas...'

After she left Sally, Star didn't go straight home, despite the fact that she had spoken the truth when she had said that she had work to do. Instead, she drove aimlessly along the country lanes outside the town, trying to bring some kind of order to her chaotic thoughts.

Even she couldn't refuse to accept that Sally had been telling her the truth. An unfamiliar feeling of panic seized her, her hands literally shaking as she held the steering wheel, a sense of foreboding and unease rushing threateningly towards her like thunderclouds in a summer sky—menacing, obscuring, gathering on the horizon.

It just wasn't possible that she had been wrong about Kyle. She couldn't have been. She knew that. All that rubbish he had mouthed about needing love and commitment, about finding sex empty and meaningless without them—it was just a clever way of tricking a woman into lowering her defences; she hadn't been wrong about that. She *couldn't* have been. Her whole body was trembling now, fear invading her like a black miasma. But fear of what?

She remembered how badly her body had ached after Kyle had left her, how she had woken at dawn with it still aching and shreds of misery-inducing dreams still lingering painfully in her mind—dreams from her childhood in which she had been left abandoned and fearful, knowing that she had done something dreadfully wrong as she cried out after the angry, disapproving faces of the adults around her, who ignored her pleas for them to remain, turning instead to leave her...to punish her.

She had rationalised her feelings, of course: her aching body had quite simply been the result of sexual frustration. It had, after all, been a long time since she had last had any sexual satisfaction and she had never been embarrassed or ashamed about acknowledging her body's needs before, she had reminded herself angrily, so why should she be so now, just because it was Kyle who had aroused her? And as for her dreams... Well the cause of those had quite obviously been the letter that she had received from her father.

She still hadn't replied to it; the letter itself had disappeared and although she couldn't actually remember doing so she imagined that she must have thrown it away. She would have to acknowledge it, of course, and with the formal 'regrets' card and a wedding-gift cheque—after all, she already knew, didn't she, that her money would be far more welcome than her actual presence? It was just as well that the rest of her commissions had gone so well recently, she decided tiredly as she turned the car around and headed for home.

Her flat seemed unusually sterile and empty after the untidy busyness of Sally's kitchen. Her friend would make a good mother, Star acknowledged—unlike her. But then Sally had Claire to model herself on, whilst she... Her mother had hardly been the maternal type and had said frequently and openly in front of Star that her life would have been much easier without the burden of a child, especially since that same child's father had managed to evade all responsibility towards her.

The issue of children had never been one which Star had given much thought to—there had been no need. She had known almost all her life that she would not have any, just as she had known that she would never commit herself to a man. Kyle, of course, would want dozens of them and would adore and dote on them.

Kyle! Angrily she cursed herself under her breath. Well, she wished him joy of them and of the woman he would marry to mother them. Star knew exactly what she would be like, of course: the complete antithesis of her—small, sweet, loved by everyone who knew her, universally praised as a perfect mother and wife, docilely content to let Kyle take the lead in every aspect of their lives and to dutifully turn a blind eye when he chose to stray from his proclaimed path of virtue. And, of course, he would stray, but not with her, Star decided savagely as she brought her car to a halt outside her apartment block. Never with her.

The phone was ringing as she opened the front door,

tantalisingly stopping just as she managed to reach it. So what? Whoever it was would no doubt ring back; in the meantime she had work to do, or rather she desperately wished she had work to do. Despite all her efforts to do so, she had not as yet been able to come up with a satisfactorily inspirational alternative to her original idea for Brad's campaign, something that enthused her sufficiently for her to feel that familiar bite of excitement that she knew she needed to bring out the best of her inventive mind.

The phone rang again. She reached for the receiver and stiffened as she heard her father's voice.

'Star…just thought I'd give you a ring to apologise again for not being able to put you and your friend up here at the house, but you know how it is. Everyone's going to be home for the wedding and we're already having problems fitting everyone in as it is. Mind you, you'll probably be far more comfortable at the George; I've booked you a suite for the night.

'We'll be having a small family dinner party here at the house on the Friday evening and of course the pair of you will be more than welcome to join us if you wish, although Kyle didn't sound too sure you would.

'Nice chap. Where did you meet him, by the way? He's obviously American… Must admit, it came as a bit of a surprise when he rang to confirm that you'd both be coming, but he explained that you were right in the middle of a big campaign—'

'Dad…' Star tried to interrupt him chokily, but she could already hear the sound of children quarrelling in the background and before she could tell her father that, whatever Kyle might have said, she had no plans to attend her stepsister's wedding he was speaking again quickly.

'Look, I must go… It's the triplets. Louise has gone out shopping and left me in charge. Look forward to seeing you both.'

'Dad…' Star tried again, this time with more desperation in her voice, but it was already too late—the line had gone dead; he had more important, more pressing matters to deal with than listening to her. When had it been any different?

Just what did Kyle think he was doing? she fumed silently as she replaced the receiver. Who did he think he was? What gave *him* the right to take it upon himself to telephone her father for *any* reason, never mind to accept an invitation that she had already decided to decline, and never mind including himself in it at the same time?

'I could come with you…' he had suggested casually, and at the time she had simply thought that he was trying to find another way of undermining her. Perhaps he still was. Why, after all, should he want to go with her?

If he had been a different man and it had been a different situation, his motives would have been obvious: a night away in a hotel would give him the ideal opportunity to try to seduce her; but, given the situation which existed between Kyle and herself, such a scenario was ludicrously laughable. Kyle would run a mile rather than put himself in a situation where there was any possibility of any kind of intimacy between the two of them; any thoughts of seduction entering his head were more likely to be centred on *his* fear that *she* might attempt to seduce *him*, rather than by any desire on his part to take advantage of her.

Take advantage! In spite of herself, Star laughed. What a thought! She couldn't imagine herself ever being in a situation where she might be the hesitant and uncertain recipient of a man's sexual intentions, the helpless, vulnerable female to his powerful sexual machismo, swept away by the force of the passion that his desire ignited within her, all fluttering pulses and eyes as she clung to him and pleaded with him for temperance.

What a farce. She had certainly never had to drag a

reluctant mate to her bed, but then she had certainly never had to be coaxed against her will either. She either wanted a man or she didn't. If she didn't, she said so, and when she did...

When she did, she took great care to make sure that she was always in control, both of herself and her partner.

Just as she had been in control with Kyle the other night, a taunting voice mocked her. So much in control in fact that just for one heart-stopping, faith-shaking moment before he had turned and left her, when the effect of what he had said to her and what he had physically done to her had been so strong, she had actually wanted... What? To beg him to stay? No, never...never!

Never! The denial was still reverberating angrily through her head half an hour later as she slammed the receiver back in its cradle, having discovered from his secretary that Kyle was out of the office and not expected back until much later in the day.

She had phoned him to demand an explanation of just why he had taken it upon himself to contact her father and announce that they—*they*, mark you, not merely she—would be attending Emily's wedding, and she was now furiously aware that without any outlet for her pent-up rage it was going to be almost impossible for her to concentrate on her work.

She could picture the wedding now: Emily looking traditionally pale and feminine, clinging to Star's father's arm as she walked down the aisle of the small village church, then the reception in a marquee at a local hotel—not, fortunately, the prestigious hotel where her father had booked them a suite. Just who was he trying to impress? Certainly not her; rather, it was a subtle underlining of her position as family outsider.

Yes, she could visualise the reception—the noise, the confusion, the busyness, the heat. She stood transfixed, her eyes widening slightly as the mental images unrolled inside her head.

Noise, heat, cross children, tired, irritable adults, a buffet table groaning with wilting food, a tearful bride, hot, screaming babies slightly too plump, middle-aged aunts with flushed faces. Ah, but how different it all could have been if only the hotel management had had the thought to install air-conditioning...

Switch to a different scene: a twenty-first birthday party—dim lights, loud music, gyrating bodies, flat drinks, discontent and complaints, overheated tempers, overheated and over-excited young men resorting to cooling themselves and their screaming girlfriends with the aid of shaken champagne bottles and the hotel's expensive ornamental indoor waterfall... Again how different it could have been.

Four hours later Star flung down her pencil, eased her aching back and flopped back in her chair. It wasn't the kind of campaign that she had originally envisaged—not quite as tongue-in-cheek or provocative—but her drawings certainly got the point across and, what was more, she acknowledged, they showed a year-round usage of Brad's air-conditioning units and not simply their necessity in hot weather.

She had even managed to accommodate Brad's requirement to bring in the superior efficiency of their installation and maintenance service by showing a game show in which Kyle's engineers came out points ahead as the clear winners in a competition with a rival organisation. And there was quite definitely nothing either smutty or sexist in any of the ads, Star decided in tired triumph.

All she had to do now was get them past Kyle. *All*... As she pushed her hair wearily off her face, she wished bitterly that she were able to go straight to Brad with her proposals, but, of course, she couldn't.

Her stomach rumbled, reminding her that she hadn't

had anything to eat since breakfast. The phone rang just as she walked into the kitchen but it was not Kyle returning her call as she had anticipated, much to her disappointment—she was still spoiling for a fight with him—but Lindsay.

'I just wanted to let you know that I won't be around for a few weeks, and also that we are going to give our marriage another try.'

Your marriage… What about your career? Star wanted to ask her, but she forced herself to hold her tongue. Obviously, she decided bitterly, Kyle's point of view meant far more to Lindsay than hers.

She would certainly not have advised the other woman to make the first move; she would have told her to let her husband do that. After all, he was the one in the wrong. All Lindsay had done was prove that she was a successful businesswoman. If her husband's pride couldn't take that, then in Star's opinion that was his problem and not Lindsay's.

After Lindsay had rung off Star tried Kyle's office number again but wasn't surprised when there was no reply. It was, after all, past seven o'clock.

She would have to wait until he returned home and tackle him then. And tackle him she certainly intended to do, because there was no way she was going to allow him to get away with his outrageous behaviour—no way at all.

It was gone ten o'clock when Kyle did eventually come in. Star saw him pull up next to her own car, but the phone rang before she could intercept him. This time it was her mother, who had heard the news about Emily's wedding and wanted to have a long moan about the situation. Star cut her short just as soon as she could. She was not really in the mood to listen to her mother's complaints; she had complaints of her own to lodge, far closer to home.

She had just replaced the receiver when she heard the

sound of Kyle's front door opening. Suspecting that he must be about to go out, she hurriedly opened her own front door, determined to stop him.

The smile he gave her was warmly disarming but Star was not deceived; he must have realised that it wouldn't be long before she discovered what he had done.

'I want to talk to you,' she told him angrily.

Her sharp ears just caught his ruefully murmured, 'Talk... That makes a change.'

It took a monumental effort for her not to respond. It infuriated her that he should somehow have managed to turn *his* refusal to have sex with her into a totally false assumption that *she* was desperate to have sex with him. There had never been anything personal in her determination to arouse him; all *she* had wanted to do was unmask him as the deceiver she knew him to be.

'If it's about the advertising campaign,' he told her quickly, checking his watch, 'I'm afraid—'

'No, it's *not* about the advertising campaign,' Star interrupted him fiercely. 'It's about—'

Downstairs someone had opened the entrance door, causing a sudden gust of wind to rattle the window on the landing and her half-open front door to slam shut.

Star frowned as the unexpected noise interrupted her and then gasped as she realised what had happened. She had been in such a hurry to intercept Kyle that she had neglected to put her door on the latch. Now it was not just closed but locked as well, with her on the wrong side of it, without her keys, without anything other than the clothes she stood up in. She looked disbelievingly at the door and then accusingly at Kyle.

'That's your fault,' she told him forcefully. 'Thanks to you, I'm locked out of my flat.'

'Thanks to me...?'

'Yes,' Star fumed. 'If you hadn't had the gall to interfere and telephone my father with that stupid message about us attending the wedding... *How* did you know where to telephone him anyway?' she demanded suspiciously, and then answered her own question, her eyes widening in disbelief as she accused him, 'You took my letter; you stole it. You—'

'Hey, hang on a minute,' Kyle interrupted her. 'I did no such thing. As it happens, I found the letter caught up in my jacket, and when I realised what it was—'

'You read it and—'

'I thought it would be a good idea to ring your father and introduce myself to him, explain what we planned to do.'

'What *we* planned to do?' Star was thoroughly outraged. '*We* planned to do nothing,' she protested bitterly.

Kyle looked pained. 'You'd already agreed that we should attend the wedding together.'

'I agreed no such thing.' Star could feel her face growing red with temper. 'You know what my father thinks now, don't you?' she almost howled in fury. 'He thinks that you and I... That we're... I'm not going,' she told him vehemently. 'You do realise, don't you, that he's booked us a suite, no less, and not two separate bedrooms?'

'Well, he did explain that they were a little short of space,' Kyle acknowledged, completely missing the point that she was trying to make. 'And, to be honest, I thought you'd prefer the hotel...'

'What I prefer is for you not to interfere in my life. You had no right. I'm *not* going. There's *no way* that you can make me,' she told him aggressively, before turning round to walk back into her own flat.

Only, of course, she couldn't, could she? She paused, mentally consigning him to the deepest, blackest depths of hell, and then gritted her teeth, turned round and told Kyle crankily, 'I need to use your phone...'

'I'm afraid you can't,' Kyle told her politely.

Star stared at him. 'What you mean, I can't? I've *got*

to. I've locked myself out of my flat, thanks to you. I need to ring a locksmith.'

'Doesn't anyone have a spare?' Kyle asked her.

'No,' Star told him. That was against the rules, of course. They were supposed to deposit a spare with a trusted key-holder, only she balked at the idea of any-one—anyone at all—having access to her most private domain and so she had never supplied one.

'I need to use your phone,' she repeated, but Kyle was adamant.

'You can't...'

'Just try stopping me,' Star challenged him angrily, marching past him and straight into his flat, where upon she came to an abrupt halt. The hall and the sitting room beyond were both completely empty.

'What's happening?' she demanded. 'Where's the fur-niture?'

'Gone,' Kyle told her ruefully. 'Apparently your late neighbours neglected to settle all their bills before they left and this morning the bailiffs arrived and removed their furniture...'

'*And* the telephone?' Star protested. 'But that's...'

Kyle shook his head. 'No, that's been cut off. Apparently they didn't pay that bill either. I've made arrangements to have it reinstated and to have new fur-niture delivered but unfortunately not until tomorrow.'

'They must have left something,' Star said weakly as she stared around the empty rooms.

'They did,' Kyle agreed. 'The bed,' he told her when she looked questioningly at him. 'I bought a new one. The one they left wasn't very comfortable.'

'The bed... That's *all* the furniture you've got...a bed...?'

'Well, they left the kitchen fitments as well,' Kyle informed her. 'So at least we can eat as well as sleep.'

'*We*?' Star glared at him. 'If you think I'm sharing a bed with you...' she began.

But Kyle reminded her, 'It's either that or the floor.'

'You've got a car,' Star pointed out. 'You could take me to a hotel.'

'I could, but I doubt that they'd allow you to book in...not dressed like that...not without any money.'

'Dressed like what?' Star glanced down at herself and realised that he did have a point. She had no shoes on, her feet were bare and she was wearing a loose, soft cotton top and an old pair of leggings—hardly the kind of apparel to inspire financial confidence.

'You could lend me some money; in fact I could stay here and *you* could book into a hotel room,' she told him.

Kyle shook his head. 'No way,' he told her firmly. 'This is my flat and my bed—a new bed, an extremely comfortable bed, a bed I am not prepared to give up for a demanding termagant who—'

'Oh, very chivalrous,' Star interrupted him, angry colour scorching her face. How dared he refer to her as a termagant? She had every right to be angry with him after what he had done.

'I could go to Sally's,' she told him.

'You could,' he agreed, looking down at her feet. 'But it's quite a long walk, at least five miles.'

Star gritted her teeth. 'You're enjoying this, aren't you?' she challenged him bitterly, and the smile that curled his mouth and his open acceptance of her accusation did nothing to alleviate her rising temper.

'Do you blame me?' he asked her drily. 'After all, would *you* turn down an opportunity to put one over on me, Star...to have me at a disadvantage? Don't perjure yourself,' he advised her kindly. 'We both already know the answer...'

He was right, of course, but that didn't make it any easier to bear. How could she have been so stupid as to forget her keys or, at the very least, to put the door on the latch? She knew how, of course: she had been in

such a steam of temper, so seriously determined to vent
her anger on him, that she hadn't stopped to think. That
nasty, niggling awareness that she was very much the
author of her own misfortune couldn't be denied—at
least, not to herself—but she was damned if she was
going to admit it to him.

'If you hadn't made that idiotic telephone call to my
father, none of this would have happened. Why did
you?' she demanded.

'I thought it was what you wanted,' he told her in-
nocently. He was playing with her, deliberately baiting
her; Star knew that.

She breathed in slowly and tried to count to ten.

'Really?' She gave him a saccharine smile, her teeth
snapping together audibly as she told him, 'I don't believe you; you're just trying to...'

'To what?' he queried. 'To do a little game-playing
of my own...a little truth-outing? Aha. You don't like it
when the boot is on the other foot, do you?' he taunted
her as he saw the way her eyes flashed.

'What do you mean, "a little truth-outing"?' Star
asked him grimly, ignoring his mockery.

'You said you wanted to have sex with me to prove
that I was lying when I said I didn't want sex without
emotion or commitment,' he reminded her.

'Yes,' Star agreed doggedly.

'Well, perhaps *I* have a little theory testing of my own
I want to put into practice.'

'Theory-testing? What kind of theory-testing?' Star
asked suspiciously.

'Well, now...' he drawled. 'I kinda think that that's
for me to know and for you to think about, don't you?'

For once Star was bereft of any suitable reply; her
mouth opened and then closed again, her temper reaching boiling point and running over it as she realised that
somehow or other he had wrestled control of the situa-

tion from her and that there wasn't a damn thing she could do about it.

'I'm not going to let you get away with this,' she warned him darkly when she had finally got her voice back. 'Whatever it is…'

To her chagrin, she saw that Kyle was actually daring to laugh at her.

'You know what you need, don't you?' he advised her solemnly. 'A cool shower, a hot drink and a good night's sleep.'

He was treating her like an overwrought child, Star recognised as she contrasted his cheerful good temper with her own impotent fury.

'What I *want*,' she told him through gritted teeth, 'is to remove you from my life…permanently and preferably immediately…'

'Ah, but, you see, you were the one who invited me into it,' Kyle reminded her.

'I invited you into my bed…not my life,' Star corrected him, determined to have the last word.

'Mmm… Well, now it's my turn to invite you into mine… What's wrong?' he asked when he saw the look that she was giving him. 'I promise you, you have nothing to fear. Your virtue is completely safe with me.'

Star glared at him. 'Don't be ridiculous,' she told him witheringly. 'And, for your information, I have *never* been afraid of a man making unwanted sexual advances to me.'

She had intended her statement to be a contemptuous put-down but somehow or other she must have missed her mark, she decided as Kyle responded gently, 'No, I don't suppose you have.'

CHAPTER EIGHT

IRRITATINGLY, Kyle had insisted that there was no way she could go to bed until she had had something to eat, and, ignominiously, Star had been so hungry that she had practically fallen on the simple meal of scrambled eggs and toast that he had made for her.

He was like a mother hen the way he fussed, Star decided waspishly now as he handed her a milky bed-time drink which she grimaced over before drinking. Not like a real man at all. Surprisingly the drink tasted delicious; she sniffed it suspiciously and accused him, 'You've put something in this, haven't you? Brandy...'

'The classic seducer's trick,' Kyle agreed solemnly, and then added, 'I'm surprised you never tried that one on me...'

'I was *not* trying to seduce you,' she reminded him. 'I simply wanted to prove...'

'Go on,' Kyle encouraged her. 'You wanted to prove...?'

'I've had enough of this,' Star told him, finishing her drink. 'I'm going to bed.'

She was undressed and in the shower before she remembered that she had nothing to sleep in—not that that would normally have bothered her; it was just that on this occasion... The thought of having to sleep in her bulky top was totally unappealing and as for her briefs... Well, she had already rinsed them out so that they would be fresh for the morning.

Wrapping a towel around her body, she went in search

of Kyle. He was in the kitchen, predictably tidying up. What a man... Just as well they hadn't had sex; it would have been bound to be a disaster...

'I need something to wear,' she told him aggressively.

His eyebrows rose.

'Such as...?'

'Something,' she insisted. 'Anything... You must have a pair of pyjamas somewhere.'

'Nope,' Kyle denied.

'But you must have... What if you had to go into hospital?'

'What an optimist,' Kyle laughed. 'The best I can do is a T-shirt.'

'I suppose it will have to do,' Star told him ungraciously, following as he went into the bedroom and pulled open a cupboard door.

The T-shirt he handed her was soft and white and extremely large. She frowned slightly, remembering how snugly she had seen a similar T-shirt fitting him. She wasn't exactly minute and yet to judge from the width of the fabric she was holding...

She saw the way Kyle was watching her and stated crossly, 'I can't put it on until you've gone.'

Infuriatingly he started to laugh.

'Now I've heard everything,' he told her. 'You're quite happy to have sex with me—an act for which, presumably, you initially remove your clothes—and yet the mere thought that I might actually see your naked body throws you into a girlish display of maidenly modesty that wouldn't disgrace a virginal sixteen-year-old. Amazing...'

'No, it isn't; it's a perfectly normal female reaction,' Star corrected him, throwing him a look of vitriolic hatred.

How dared he laugh at her? How dared he... How dared he...how dared he *exist*? she fumed a few minutes later when he had gone, leaving her free to drop her damp towel and pull on his T-shirt. It was enormous on her. It was probably one he deliberately kept to impress women, she decided balefully. It was probably enormous on him too.

She yawned sleepily and burrowed deeper into her pillow. How much brandy had he actually put in that drink? she wondered. She yawned again, her body starting to relax. He had been right about one thing: this bed...*his* bed...was blissfully comfortable.

Well, she looked as though she was asleep, Kyle decided fifteen minutes later, cautiously opening the bedroom door. She ought to be; he had given her enough brandy to knock out a horse—an invidious tactic, but it was either that or risk spending the whole night with her arguing with him. What a woman.

He padded silently to the bathroom and stripped off his clothes before turning on the shower.

He wondered how long it would be before she guessed what he was up to. There was no need to question what her reaction would be when she did. He was playing a mite unfairly, he had to admit that, but then desperate needs called for desperate measures and he was certainly desperate. Any man would have to be to get involved in what he was getting himself involved in, but he was determined to show her that her antagonism towards his sex sprang not from the conviction she clung so determinedly and defensively to—that none of his sex could be trusted—but rather from her fear of the pain she had experienced when her father had left.

Once he could show her that with him she had nothing to fear... That his feelings...his love... That *he* would always... Hang on there, he warned himself. There was still a hell of a lot of ground to cover before she was ready to listen to that kind of talk from him—one hell of a long way to go.

He looked down into her sleeping face and somehow

managed to resist the temptation to kiss the tip of her
nose before throwing back the covers and quietly sliding
into bed beside her—alongside her. Alongside, when
what he would have preferred to do...where he would
have preferred to be... Determinedly, he closed his eyes.

Star smiled happily in her sleep and snuggled closer to
the male body lying alongside her own. Mmm...it felt
so delicious...all that warm, soft, furry male body hair
against her skin, and that lovely, tantalisingly erotic man
smell—so totally unfamiliar...and yet somehow, deep
down inside herself, she instinctively and immediately
recognised a sense of being safe and warm and wanted,
had an awareness of the rightness of being where she
was and with whom she was.

She made a soft sound of pleasure and burrowed even
closer to the source of all those wonderful feel-good sensations and emotions whilst Kyle held his breath.

He had woken up fifteen minutes ago, alerted to Star's
unconscious "sleepwalk" across the gap that he had left
between them by the unmistakable physical response of
his own body to her proximity. For once, he was able
to acquit her of any attempt to manipulate or manoeuvre
him—*she* was quite definitely deeply asleep—and if he
hadn't been finding it so damned hard to hold onto his
self-control, or if he'd been a different type of man, he
could have been giving himself a little bit of congratu-
lation at the way Star's sleeping expression and her
small sounds of pleasure betrayed how much she was
enjoying her unwitting physical contact with his body.

His body or just any male body? Kyle frowned. Despite everything he had heard about her and everything
she had told him about herself, Kyle had guessed that
emotionally, where it really counted, Star was completely untried and untouched—virginal in that in her
previous relationships she had always withheld her real,
deep, inner self. And, as he had already told her, that

kind of shallow pseudo-intimacy could never be enough
for him. He held his breath as she burrowed even closer
against him.

If this carried on much longer…! It had been difficult
enough for him to resist her when she'd been deliberately and cold bloodedly trying to arouse him, but what
she was doing now, with that sweetly sensual look of
desire on her sleeping face… If she moved against him
like that just one more time…

Kyle knew that he was audibly grinding his teeth as
she still tried to get closer, pushing his arm out of the
way, a small pout puckering her mouth as she tugged
on his hand. Obediently he raised it and then dropped it
again as he realised what he was doing, but somehow
or other his hand had already found the smooth curve
of her hip, and once there it was impossible for him to
resist the temptation to stroke her skin, so soft and warm
and alive, so womanly and desirable…so…so Star.

Outside the birds had started to sing. Star's pout dis-
solved into a dazzling smile as she rubbed her face
against his chest, appreciatively breathing in his scent,
nuzzling him and making soft, murmuring, cooing
sounds of pleasure.

A man would have to be a saint to remain unaffected
by what she was doing, Kyle acknowledged achingly.
No studied, practised, deliberately calculated seduction
could have had one tenth of the effect on him that her
instinctive, artless, innocent betrayal of her desire to be
close to him was now.

Somehow or other his gentle fingertip-touch against
her skin had become a slow, lingering, rhythmic caress
that had found the delicate, narrow indentation of her
waist and moved beyond it to the full, rounded curve of
her breast, just made to fit perfectly within the cup of
his hand.

Star gave a softly voluptuous sigh and arched her
spine. Kyle groaned out loud. Star was touching him

now, exploring the hard muscles of his back and moving lower, whilst the soft warmth of her breathing against his throat quickened. Against the hand that covered her breast he could feel her nipple swell and harden, just as his body was doing—just as it had been doing from the moment she'd started to move closer to him.

Reluctantly Kyle released her breast and started to ease her away from him gently, bending his head to kiss her forehead tenderly as he did so, only Star wouldn't let him go. Her hands clung to his shoulders and she was moving her body so that she was as close to him as it was possible to be, one long, slim leg wrapping itself firmly around him so that...

Kyle could feel the heat burning up under his skin as the T-shirt he had lent her rode up and he felt the warm, silky, bare length of her thigh pressing against him. He reached out, intending only to move her.

It was more than any man could be expected to stand...*any* man. With a smothered groan, Kyle gathered her closer, one hand sliding up under the T-shirt as he held her, the other lifting to push the soft mass of her hair off her face and slide along her jaw, cupping it lovingly as he bent his head to kiss her.

He kissed her once, very gently and delicately, a second time for no better reason than the fact that her mouth tasted so sweet and he was so hungry for her that he just couldn't resist it, and then a third time, deeper and longer, because, well, if a man was going to damn himself he might as well do the job properly, mightn't he?

Of course he might, and of course Star woke up. How could she not do?

Star was not in the habit of dreaming about being made love to and certainly not about the kind of lovemaking that included delicious, tantalising half-kisses that touched and awoke and inflamed her senses more intensely and erotically than any real, experienced kiss she could ever remember.

She didn't like having such dreams and, more specifically, she didn't like having such dreams about the one man who was least likely to want to participate in them with her. They made her feel angry and cheated...and...and vulnerable, as though there was something missing from her life—which was ridiculous; how could there be anything missing from the life that she had specifically and deliberately chosen and tailored for herself? Of course there couldn't be.

She tried to say the words out loud—a sure-fire mantra which had never failed to work in the past—only this time she couldn't actually say the words because something...someone was making it impossible for her to do so. Someone was kissing her; someone was...

Star opened her eyes and then closed them again on a dizzy wave of disbelief. Kyle was kissing her. Kyle was holding her. Kyle was lying so close to her that she could feel every single movement of his body against her own, every breath he took...every beat of his pulse... Every beat of his pulse...? Impossible. 'Impossible!'

She said the word quite clearly as Kyle lifted his mouth from hers in anticipation of her furious demand for an explanation of what he thought he was doing. And then he realised that no such demand was going to come, that she had in fact closed her eyes and snuggled back into his arms with a sigh of pure, feminine, seductive bliss, following her instincts and reaching up towards him, her hand on his jaw as she lifted her head off the pillow to close the small distance between them, her lips unexpectedly hesitant and searching as they caressed his own—more questioning than demanding, Kyle recognised as he kissed her back, his tongue tracing the shape of her mouth.

The immediate shudder of response that convulsed her

body surprised them both, Star's body tensing, her eyes opening as she waited warily.

She didn't like being responsive to him, Kyle sensed. Her body language told him that she wanted him to let her go, but he refused to respond to it.

'What's wrong?' he asked her softly. 'I thought this was what you wanted...to prove...'

'I've changed my mind,' Star snapped back at him, suddenly wide awake and made antagonistic by her realisation of what was happening to her and how vulnerable she felt. She was never the one to become so quickly and so intensely aroused—certainly not by a mere kiss. The sensation of wanting to be close to him...of wanting him...was alien and unfamiliar to her and she was afraid of it.

'Let me go,' she demanded tautly. 'I don't want—'

'You don't want what?' Kyle interrupted her softly. 'Me?'

He raised his hand and cupped the side of her breast, letting the tip of his thumb just touch the erect crest of her nipple whilst he told her gently, 'Liar.'

It was a case of being cruel to be kind, he told himself in justification of the stricken, panicky expression that he could see darkening her eyes. Instinct told him that she had never been in a situation like this before, never known what it was like to be afraid of her own sexuality.

Whilst she watched him her hands curled into two small, tense fists. Kyle bent his head and very gently kissed the centre of each breast, one after the other, his caress leaving the fine cotton fabric of his T-shirt clinging moistly to her skin.

He had never previously thought that there was anything particularly erotic about the sight of a girl wearing a wet T-shirt that was clinging to her otherwise naked breasts, but now, suddenly, there was a sensation inside him that was all male and entirely primitive. Before Star could stop him he had bent his head to her body again

and this time there was no way she could control her
fevered response to the sensation of his mouth dragging
the slightly abrasive, damp fabric against the sensitivity
of her skin.

Given that cerebrally the last thing she wanted was
for him to continue what he was doing, it was perhaps
a trifle contradictory for Star to give a little smothered
gasp of pleasure and arch her body up against his mouth
in deliberate incitement of a continuation of his mouth's
sensual destruction of her self-control.

Star clutched at Kyle's shoulders, her nails digging
into the hard muscle as wave upon wave of barely en-
durable pleasure swamped her. She was a sensual, sexual
woman who had thought that she understood her body
and was familiar with all of its responses, but this…!

This aching, overwhelming need was something else
again and, as she had with everything else in her life
which had made her feel threatened and vulnerable, Star
fought against it, frantically trying to push Kyle away as
his hands lifted her T-shirt and his mouth moved from
her breasts to her ribcage and then lower, gently caressing and arousing every single inch of her skin.

Male desire, male urgency, male hunger—all of these
she was used to, all of them gave her power and weak-
ened the man who exhibited them. Male tenderness,
male gentleness, male desire to give her pleasure—these
were alien to her and she was both angered and frightened by them. They overwhelmed her, undermined her,
made her want to reach out and hold onto the man caressing her, made her want to cling to him, to give the
real essence of herself to him, and Star had never given
anything of herself to any man, not since her father had
abandoned her, not since she had realised that giving
your love to a man meant being hurt by him.

Her love!

Star froze, the only movement in her body the small
ripple of sensation just under her skin where Kyle's

mouth had been slowly caressing the smooth curve of
her hip.

But she didn't love Kyle.

This need she could feel battling with her brain's
fierce exhortation to her to push him away, to make herself safe, this desire to reach out and touch him, to feel
his skin beneath her hands, her mouth, to hold him and
wrap herself around him, to draw him deep, deep within
her body and to hold him there—all this was nothing…
It meant nothing. How could it when *he* meant nothing?

His fingertips stroked sensually along the inside of her
thigh. How could she ever have thought that his refusal
to touch her must mean that he was somehow sexually
inadequate? she wondered. This man could do more to
arouse her senses to a fever pitch of aching need with a
single kiss, a single touch, than any other man had been
able to using every kind of sophisticated foreplay that
had ever been imagined.

His mouth trailed moistly along her hip-bone, following the fierce pulse-beat of need that was beginning to
throb through her whole body.

He was, Star witnessed, as unconcerned about her
viewing his own arousal as he was concerned about en-
suring that she experienced every single sensation of her
own.

In the dawn light she could see his body perfectly
clearly through the sharply painful glitter of the tears
which had, for some reason, filled her eyes and blocked
her throat.

His body was everything that a man's body should
be—well muscled without in any way becoming a caricature of over-developed and somehow totally non-
sexual maleness, his skin warmed by the sun but not
over-tanned, his body hair darkly silky, heart-lurchingly
male both to her sight and her touch.

She wanted to reach out to him as she had never
wanted to reach out to any other man, to touch him with

her fingertips and her mouth, to know and explore him—
not clinically and cold-bloodedly, with the single-
minded purpose of arousing him, but for her own pleasure as well as for his and because she actually wanted
the feel and the taste of him beneath her hands and her
mouth. Oh, how she wanted them. Oh, how she wanted
them…and him.

Star closed her eyes to block not just the weakness of
her tears but, even more importantly, the sight of so
much temptation.

But nothing could block out her senses, her
mind…her heart, her vulnerability and the root cause of
it.

'Stop it… I don't want this.'

Kyle heard the words but it took several seconds for
their actual meaning to sink through the fierce thrill of
aroused pleasure that the sensation of Star's wonderfully
warm and responsive body beneath his mouth gave him.
Every touch, every caress, every soft drift of his mouth
released a small, frantic torrent of responsive quivers and
movement. He had never known a woman so warmly
and vibrantly alive, so sensually aware. Just holding her
and touching her the way he was doing right now was
more deeply, sensually pleasurable for him than any
lovemaking he had known in the past.

The thought of how she would feel, how she would
be when he eventually reached the hot, sweet heart of
her was already making his heart pound with deep,
heavy hammer-blows of surging longing.

He would take his time, draw out the moment of pleasure, kiss and caress every tiny bit of her, touch her
gently with his tongue in that special, sensual and oh,
so sensitive place, waiting until she was ready for him
before taking her fully into his mouth and feeling her
body dissolve in liquid waves of sensual release.

But she was telling him that she didn't want that. That

she didn't want him. Reluctantly Kyle responded to her rejection, her denial.

The moment he released her Star scrambled off the bed. Her legs were shaking so much that she could barely stand up. She felt sick and anxious and angrily frightened as well...

'No,' she said loudly, her body going rigid as she fought to reject her emotions. Kyle, who had been about to reach out to her, let his hand drop back to his side.

'I rang you several times this morning but there was no reply.'

'No, there wouldn't be. I wasn't there,' Star told her mother shortly.

It was less than an hour since she had finally managed to get into her flat with the aid of a locksmith who had exchanged the kind of knowing male look with Kyle when she had explained her predicament that set her teeth on edge.

And, of course, the commotion they'd caused had brought Amy out to see what was going on, and Star had been well aware of what was going through her mind when she had asked where Star had spent the night and Kyle had responded immediately, 'With me.'

Although why she should care or feel angry and self-conscious she had no idea...she told herself. Only, of course, she did, just as she knew exactly why she was so reluctant to explain to her mother what had happened.

It had nothing to do with any kind of embarrassment or guilt over the fact that she had spent the night with a man and everything to do with her own illogical behaviour and emotions. Even now she still couldn't believe what she had done. She, a woman who had always prided herself on being in control of her sexuality, for some totally inexplicable reason had suddenly become so overwhelmed by it, so afraid of it that she had had to take refuge in the kind of female behaviour that she had thought belonged solely to nervous young virgins.

No woman of her experience *ever* let things get to the stage that she had done and then said no. No woman...but she had. And not because she had suddenly had a change of heart and decided that she didn't want Kyle. Oh, no. Certainly not because of that... If only!

A change of heart! Star closed her eyes and tried to swallow past the huge, painful lump which had blocked her throat. How very appropriate that she should pick on such a phrase... How appropriate and how appalling...

'Star...? Star, are you still there?'

'Yes, I'm still here, Mother,' she responded huskily, dimly aware that her mother was in the midst of complaining about Emily's wedding again, but too preoccupied with her own thoughts to try to stop her.

'I was just wondering why on earth your father's making such a thing about Emily's marriage. It isn't even as though she is his child. Of course, he always did enjoy throwing her in my face...the child of the woman he discarded me for...making it obvious that she took precedence over you...'

Star sighed. She had heard it all so many, many times before. 'Perhaps he genuinely did prefer her to me,' she pointed out quietly to her mother. 'After all, she was...is...far more the kind of daughter he wanted.'

'Rubbish... He just did it to spite me. Well, it's just as well he didn't invite me. I couldn't have gone. As a matter of fact...'

Star frowned as her mother's voice faltered betrayingly.

'Well, I might as well tell you now... I shall be getting married myself. Very quietly, *very* quietly,' she stressed. 'And we'll actually be away on honeymoon the day Emily gets married.'

Star took a deep breath.

'I see,' she said as neutrally as she could as she tried

not to visualise her mother standing side by side with
the gangly, still not fully grown teenager who was her
current lover, making what in Star's opinion was a total
mockery of the sacred vows of marriage.

'And Iris... Has she become reconciled to you and
Mark marrying or—?'

'Mark!' Her mother's response was immediate and
shocked. 'Don't be ridiculous, Star. I'm not marrying
Mark; he's only a boy, a child...'

Not marrying Mark. Hard on the heels of her relief
Star felt her stomach start to churn with the familiar
sensation of anger and anxiety that her mother so often
caused.

'Not Mark,' she repeated slowly. 'Then who are you
marrying, Mother?'

'Why, Brian, of course,' her mother responded impatiently, for all the world as though Star were a particularly dense child. 'Who else?'

Who else indeed? Star opened her mouth to remind
her mother of all the other 'who elses' there could have
and had been and then closed it again.

Brian Armstrong was one of her mother's oldest
friends. He had known her before she had met and married Star's father and he had remained patiently and, so
far as Star was concerned, unfathomably devoted to her
in all the years since.

Whenever her mother was in trouble it was Brian she
turned to. He was her rock, her one true friend, she had
once laughingly told him in Star's presence, and Star,
eight years old then, seeing the painful way he blushed
and looked away, had been torn with embarrassment at
witnessing such intense adult emotion and anger at her
mother for causing it and for being oblivious and uncaring of what she was doing.

Brian had loved her mother for as long as Star could
remember, but never once had her mother given any
indication that she might return that emotion.

'Brian,' she said numbly. 'But Mother—'

'I know what I'm doing, Star,' her mother interrupted her firmly. 'I should have married him years ago but I suppose I wanted to show…to prove to your father that he wasn't the only one who could change partners whenever the mood suited him… I saw him not long ago, you know… He had those three children with him—the triplets… He looked so old… Poor man… I almost felt sorry for him.

'Brian and I are getting married in the Caribbean, by the way,' she told Star. 'So romantic… It's time *you* got married, Star,' her mother reproved her. 'I can just imagine how Louise will be crowing over the fact that her daughter is getting married first.'

'Mother…' Star started to protest warningly, but her mother was already announcing that she had to go and replacing the receiver.

Her mother remarrying…again. Well, at least she was marrying Brian and not Mark, Star reflected, which was probably the most sensible, the *only* sensible decision that her mother had made in her entire life.

Unlike her mother's, all *her* decisions were sensible and well thought out. She never acted on her emotions, nor allowed them to rule her. Never…

'And Kyle asked me to ask if you could come in to see him and bring whatever work you've managed to do on the campaign so far,' Star heard Tim's secretary explaining to her as she cradled the telephone receiver against her ear.

'Well, I haven't really got very much to show him as yet,' Star said untruthfully.

But Mrs Hawkins had obviously been primed by Kyle not to accept any put-offs, because she insisted, with quiet firmness, 'He has a free slot this afternoon at four and I know he's hoping to fly home this weekend to report to Brad.'

To fly home. Kyle was going to be away... How long for? Just...just for the weekend or for longer...? Star didn't like the ominous way her heart lurched and then started to beat far too fast. Kyle had said nothing to her about being away.

But then, why should he?

'I'll try to make it for four.' She gave in unwillingly. It wasn't that she didn't have anything to show Kyle, she acknowledged ten minutes later as she started to gather together her new story-boards. She did. And it wasn't even that she was afraid of him rejecting her work. So what was she so afraid of, then? Kyle himself? Why should she be?

Her face burned as she recalled exactly why she felt so reluctant to face him. How could she account for her ignominious flight from his bed this morning? After all the things she had said to him...all the taunts...all the insults...that *she* should be the one to cry craven, to say stop... And why had she?

She shook her head, still not ready to answer that question, even to herself.

'Kyle will see you now.'

Star squared her shoulders and nodded tersely in acknowledgement of Mrs Hawkins's statement as she stood up and gathered her work together.

As Star headed towards Kyle's office his secretary reflected that she looked as though she was about to undergo a gruelling ordeal, rather like her own dreaded visits to her dentist, and yet, personally, Mrs Hawkins found working for Kyle one of the most serendipitous experiences of her entire working life. He had that American way with him of somehow getting things done, of removing obstacles and barriers almost instantaneously and yet, at the same time, always remaining calm and polite.

Tim was a lovely man, of course, gentle and thoughtful, but he *had* lacked Kyle's resolution, his ability to insist on high standards and good workmanship. Mrs Hawkins had noticed already the drop in complaints from their customers, just as she had noted and approved of the firm way in which some of their less than efficient fitters and technicians had been dealt with and the way far more stringent standards and checks had been established for those who had taken their place.

Kyle reached the door before Star did, opening it for her and ushering her inside, watching her gravely.

How on earth was she supposed to concentrate on her work, Star wondered wretchedly, when all she could remember, all she could think about was that this morning she had been in Kyle's bed, had lain in his arms, and his touch had taught her things about herself that she had never dreamed existed—things she wished passionately that she had not discovered existed?

How could she concentrate on her work when she was still trying to deal with the aftershock of those discoveries?

'I've rewritten the proposed advertising copy, taking into account your criticisms,' she began stiffly as she lined up the story-boards.

Even with her back to him, she could sense Kyle moving closer to her to study what she had done. Quickly she moved out of the way. Kyle had stopped in front of the first board and was examining it. Making sure she kept a safe distance between them, Star waited until he had examined all of them.

'I like it... It's very good,' he told her when he had finished.

'It doesn't have the same punch as the other ideas,' Star asserted.

'No, perhaps not,' Kyle agreed. 'It *is* gentler, less hard-hitting, but in my opinion that won't detract from its overall impact.

'Don't forget that in the main we're selling these systems to men, not women, and most men, although they might be loath to admit it, do feel intimidated by and are antagonistic to what they see as domineering or aggressive women—women in control of themselves and their own lives...'

'Now who's being sexist?' Star couldn't resist saying grimly.

'I didn't say those were *my* feelings,' Kyle pointed out.

'Your father rang me this afternoon, by the way,' he told her in a different voice. 'He wanted to check that we were definitely going to the wedding. He said he'd tried to ring you but that you were engaged.'

Star stiffened.

'What did you say?'

Kyle shrugged. 'I confirmed that we were going and—'

'What?' Star demanded in disbelief. 'You can't possibly want to go.'

'No? How could *you* know what I might want, Star?' Kyle asked her drily. '*You* don't even know what you want yourself.'

Star stood and stared at him. She could feel the blood draining out of her face and then flooding back into it again in a hot burning tide of self-conscious colour and she knew that she couldn't do a damn thing about it or what it betrayed about her.

'That's not true,' she managed to deny unevenly, and then, unable to bear it any longer, she moistened her suddenly dry lips with the tip of her tongue and told him angrily, 'That's typical of a man... Just because a woman says no when she...'

'When she means yes, or rather—'

'I did not mean yes,' Star denied. 'How dare you imply that I did? That's the oldest trick in the book so far as your sex is concerned—claiming that you know a woman means yes when she says no and using that as an excuse to force her—'

'*I* didn't force you to do anything, Star,' Kyle pointed out gently. 'I do understand, you know,' he told her softly. 'I know you were afraid—'

'Afraid?' Star tensed. 'What have I got to be afraid of?' she demanded acidly. Her eyebrows rose mockingly. 'You?'

Kyle cursed himself under his breath. He had said too much but he had spent the whole damn day thinking about her, worrying about her, wanting to go to her and yet guessing how she would react if he did. And he had been right. But, tempted as he was to let her off the hook, to make it easy for her, he couldn't let himself lose the small piece of ground he had won, for her sake as well as his own.

'No, not me,' he acknowledged. 'What you fear, Star, is yourself, or rather your own emotions. That's what you're afraid of—needing someone, wanting someone...*loving* someone...'

'Loving someone!' Star exploded scornfully. 'Oh, come on...please...'

She managed to make her mouth curl in a creditable display of contempt, but inside she was shaking so much that she dared not close her mouth in case her teeth started to chatter.

Panic—something she had spent virtually all her life suppressing and hiding from others—suddenly overwhelmed her and snapped the bonds she had used to tether it as easily and mockingly as the Incredible Hulk bursting out of his shirt. The incongruity, the ludicrousness of it should have made her laugh; instead she felt half-paralysed with terror.

'I'm flying out to the States on Friday,' she heard Kyle adding casually, just as though those few hauntingly destructive sentences had never been spoken. 'Why don't you come with me and we can take these—'

he pointed to the story-boards '—with us to show Brad? He'll be keen to see what you've come up with while he's been away on honeymoon.'

'No...'

The panic hadn't just escaped into her body, it had escaped into her voice as well, Star recognised as she fought to control it.

'I...I can't,' she stressed shakily. 'I...I've got some other work I need to do...'

'All weekend?' Kyle queried.

'I don't work nine to five,' Star snapped back at him. 'If something urgent comes up—'

'Of course,' Kyle agreed soothingly, walking past her to his desk, where he picked up his diary and, to her consternation, told her cheerfully after studying it, 'Well, it doesn't matter. I can reschedule my trip for after your sister's wedding, to fit in with you. Do you have your diary with you?'

'No, I don't,' Star told him through gritted teeth. 'And she is *not* my sister.'

'But she is a part of your family, and your father is still your father.'

'I'm not going to the wedding,' Star told him determinedly.

Kyle gave her a tolerant smile. 'Of course you're going,' he told her in a kindly voice, adding more firmly, 'We're *both* going. Now, about this campaign... I'd like for Brad to see what you've come up with as soon as possible.'

'Then why don't you take the story-boards with you this weekend? I could redraw everything on a small scale if you—'

'Fine,' Kyle agreed. 'I'll let Brad see this first version then I'm sure he will want to go through the whole thing with you himself,' he added. 'Could you also come up with some idea of the kind of scheduling and media scope you envisage using for the campaign?'

'A TV slot would have the greatest impact,' Star told him, 'but of course it would be expensive...'

'Mmm...I guess it would, but if it were timed to fit in with us getting into place the new fitting and technical people we're subcontracting to... Leave it with me. I'll have a word with Brad about that whilst I'm over there—'

He broke off as the phone rang, excusing himself as he went to pick it up. As he answered his call Star started to gather together her work but even though she wasn't deliberately listening she couldn't avoid hearing the warmly excited female voice exclaiming in a transatlantic accent, 'Kyle, I've just heard that you're coming home! That's wonderful. You can be sure there'll be a warm—a very warm—welcome waiting for you...'

Star could hear Kyle clearing his throat before he said quietly, 'I'm not sure exactly what time I'll be flying in and so—'

There was a giggle and then Star heard her saying, 'Well, that's OK. After all, I've still got my key...'

Picking up the last of her story-boards, Star gave him a bitterly corrosive glare before opening the door and walking through it.

It was obvious that some women...some relationships were exempt from his proclaimed desire for emotional commitment and intimacy. Unless...

She stopped abruptly in the outer office and frowned so horribly that Mrs Hawkins wondered uneasily just what on earth was wrong.

Unless the woman at the other end of the telephone was someone special, someone whom Kyle *did* want to make a full commitment to...

Well, if she was, then what the hell had he been doing in bed with *her*? Star wondered angrily as she stamped out of the office and headed for her car.

CHAPTER NINE

'KYLE came round last night. He wanted to know if we had any messages for him. He's flying out to the States today.'

'I know,' Star told Sally shortly in a tone that warned her that it wasn't a subject she wanted to pursue.

But Sally either didn't pick up on that warning or chose to ignore it, because she continued, 'Oh, heavens, I nearly forgot—Kyle asked me to remind you that the two of you have still got to sort out a wedding present for Emily. Is there anything you want to tell me?' she asked mock-innocently.

'Nothing,' Star denied.

'I see,' Sally commented judiciously. 'One moment you detest the man so much that you can't stand the sight of him, the next he's going to Emily's wedding with you...'

'It was an accident...a mistake,' Star protested crossly. 'I told him there was no need for him to interfere, to get involved, but he wouldn't listen and now there's no way I can get out of going without looking... If I back out now, everyone is bound to think that it's because I'm jealous of Emily...because she was always Dad's favourite...'

'You mean because she always made a point of making *sure* she was his favourite,' Sally corrected her roundly. 'I've never been able to understand why men are so blind to that kind of manipulation and false flattery.'

'Haven't you?' Star asked her sardonically. 'It isn't their eyesight that's the problem, it's their ego.'

'Mmm... Well, as for people thinking you're jealous of Emily, she was always the one who was jealous of you. Why else do you think she made such a big thing of ingratiating herself with your father?' Sally challenged her when Star started to shake her head.

'She's everything that I'm not—the kind of daughter that Dad always wanted. Not that it really matters now,' she said.

'Mum's getting married again, by the way,' she added, and rolled her eyes slightly as she told Sally, 'In the Caribbean and to Brian, of all men.'

'Brian? Oh, but he'll be perfect for her,' Sally enthused. 'He'll spoil her and look after her—and you'll be able to stop worrying about her and don't pretend that you don't. I know you too well,' Sally challenged her. 'You know, your father really does have a lot to answer for, Star,' she told her more gently.

'Yeah... Me for starters,' Star mocked back.

But Sally shook her head and continued firmly, 'You know that wasn't what I meant. He caused both you and your mother a lot of pain; he—'

'Mmm...well, that's men for you.' Star shrugged cynically.

'No.' Sally corrected her, 'That's *some* men, I agree; some men *are* vain and egotistical and uncaring of the hurt they inflict on others, the damage they do to other people's lives, but then so are some women. Not all men are like your father, Star,' Sally told her. 'Look at Chris...and James...and Brad...and Brian. Look at the way he's gone on loving your mother—'

'Aren't you omitting someone from this list of supermen?' Star asked her wryly. 'Kyle,' she prompted, when Sally looked puzzled. 'Surely you weren't going to miss an opportunity to point out to me what a truly wonderful, caring, sincere specimen of male perfection he is? If I were Chris I think I might be getting rather worried.'

'Chris knows he doesn't have to worry about me falling for another man,' Sally retorted firmly. 'When is Emily actually getting married?' she asked.

'Next month,' Star told her.

'Mmm…a September bride… Have you decided what you're going to wear yet?'

'I haven't a clue,' Star informed her in a voice that said that she didn't really care.

'Doing anything interesting this weekend?' Sally asked her, changing the subject.

'Nothing,' Star told her. Kyle would be doing something interesting, though. Kyle would be doing something extremely interesting; at least, he would be if the owner of that husky, feminine transatlantic voice had anything to do with it.

Kyle—why on earth was she wasting her time thinking about him? And why on earth had she been so stupid as to give in to that ridiculous and unnecessary fit of panic the other morning, when, if she'd stayed, she could have proved beyond any shadow of a doubt that she had been right about him all along?

And what had he meant anyway by that comment he had made to her about doing some truth-outing of his own? What truth-outing exactly? What truth was there to come out, after all? None… None.

And of course she wasn't missing him… Why on earth should she be? He had only been gone a matter of hours, and even if he had been gone days… months…years…it wouldn't have made any difference—she still wouldn't miss him, she insisted to herself several hours later as she padded barefoot around her flat and tried to convince herself that the reason she was trying to work out the time difference between here and North America was simply in case Brad should try to get in touch with her to discuss her work.

In case *Brad* should try to get in touch with her, she emphasised mentally for the benefit of that small, jeering, disbelieving voice which refused to let her off the hook. For no other reason.

In America Kyle opened his front door and smiled lovingly at the small, dark-haired woman who was waiting for him, opening his arms wide to receive her as she hurled herself into them.

'And how's my favourite big brother?' she asked him teasingly when he finally put her down.

'Your only big brother,' Kyle reminded her drily.

She was the youngest of his father's second family and a gap of over ten years separated them, but she was the closest in looks and temperament to her aunt, his stand-in mother, and he would have loved her just for that if for nothing else.

'You've lost weight,' she accused him, 'and you're not smiling—not properly, with your eyes. Something's wrong. What is it?'

'Nothing—there's nothing wrong,' Kyle denied, but she shook her head.

'Yes, there is. What is it...*who* is it? Who is she?' She pounced on him with awesome female instinct, adding as she saw his face, 'Aha, so it is someone... A woman... *The* woman,' she guessed triumphantly. 'Who is she, Kyle? Do I know her?'

'No,' he told her, shaking his head, and added under his breath, 'And, the way things are looking, I doubt that you ever will.'

He hadn't intended her to hear him but she had and now she was by his side, frowning her disapproval and her scorn of any woman fool enough not to want her adored elder brother.

'Want to talk about it?' she offered, but Kyle shook his head.

He had Star backed into a corner and, like any cor-

nered creature, she was desperately looking for an escape and wildly angry with it. Perhaps the kindest thing
to do would be to give her that escape. But to what? He
knew that he loved her and he was pretty certain that
she felt something for him—something that wasn't just
lust, even though he knew quite well that *she* would
claim that it was.

He had a strong suspicion that her sister's wedding
could prove to be the catalyst that pushed things one
way or the other, that removed the barriers between them
or re-erected them and made them even stronger.

He had unashamedly badgered Sally for as much information as she could give him about Star and her relationship with the rest of her family, and most especially her father, and he thought he understood just why
Star was so afraid of allowing herself to love anyone,
why she couldn't even allow herself to accept that such
a concept as love could exist between a man and a
woman.

Getting her to relinquish the shield of bitterness and
rejection that she had forged to protect herself would be
a painful process—for both of them. After all, what right
did he have to interfere in her life?

'Tell me about her,' Kelly tried to coax him, but Kyle
shook his head again. He knew his half-sister meant well
but there were some things that were too private...too
potentially painful to discuss with anyone.

His body, his brain, his mind might be here in North
America, he acknowledged, but his heart, his emotions,
his real, true essence were all in England with Star, and
that was something that was too intimate, too personal
to tell anyone. That could only be shared with one other
person. Only she didn't want to hear... She was too
afraid to let herself hear, he corrected himself tiredly.

'Hey, come back; you were miles away,' Sally accused
Star. They were having lunch together in their favourite

Italian restaurant and Sally had been regaling Star with the latest gossip when she had suddenly realised that Star was staring absently into space.

'Anyone would think you were in love,' Sally teased her.

'In love? *Me*? Don't be ridiculous,' Star retorted witheringly. But, curiously for Star, her face had suddenly become slightly flushed, Sally noted, and she couldn't quite look her in the eye.

Coincidentally Sally and Poppy had been discussing Star only the previous evening, Poppy laughing about the vow she and Claire and Star had made never get married.

'You've had two successes,' she had reminded Sally, 'but I doubt that you're going to get a third. Not with Star.'

Sally wasn't so sure, but she had kept her thoughts to herself.

'Have you heard anything from Kyle?' she asked Star conversationally now. 'I know he had to extend his stay in North America because Claire mentioned it the last time she rang.'

'No, I haven't. Why should I?' Star responded tersely. 'There's no reason why he should get in touch with me.'

'No, of course not,' Sally agreed soothingly. 'I just thought he might have rung to...to ask you to keep an eye on his flat...'

Star looked suspiciously into her friend's too innocent face but decided not to pursue the subject—not to think about the empty flat and the oddly painful feeling she had experienced the morning she had woken up and discovered that Kyle had not, as she had expected, returned. And she certainly didn't want to think about the betraying phone call she had made to Mrs Hawkins later on that same morning.

But why should she feel uncomfortable about making a phone call—an enquiry about the whereabouts of

someone whom she was, after all, involved with in a
business capacity? It was a perfectly normal and ac-
ceptable thing to do. Naturally, she needed to know
when Kyle was likely to return since he was the person
she had to channel her work through.

She didn't tell Sally any of this, though, and neither
did she tell her about the shaming way she had been
rushing straight to her answering machine to check her
messages every time she had been out, just in case Kyle
had rung.

In love. Her! The very idea was ridiculous, derisi-
ble...laughable... So why wasn't she laughing?

Star could see the light flashing on her answering machine unit as she opened her workroom door, but she
deliberately refused to go and check it until she had removed her coat and made herself a cup of coffee—like
a child forcing herself to wait and not open the most
special and exciting birthday present until last.

Coffee-mug in one hand, she sat down and ran the
tape. Her heart jolted against her ribs, coffee spilling
down onto the desk as her hand started to tremble, but
when she replayed the answering machine tape it was
Brad's voice she heard and not Kyle's.

Brad wanted her to call back so that they could discuss her campaign.

Star put down her coffee mug and walked over to the
window. Her throat ached and for some reason she found
it difficult to swallow. The familiar view outside had
become oddly hazy and misty, but it wasn't until she
blinked that she realised that her eyes had filled with
tears.

Tears. Her! And for a man? Why? What was so special about *this* man that he could have this effect on her,
that he could make her feel...want...need him in all the
ways she had promised herself she would never allow
herself to want or need any member of his sex?

She gave a small shiver. Had she been a different kind of woman she might almost have been tempted to believe that there was, after all, something in that old superstition about catching the bride's bouquet. But it was all total rubbish, of course, and the kind of outdated mythology that had no place in a modern woman's thinking or her life.

She went back to her desk and picked up the telephone receiver and quickly dialled Brad's number.

Twenty minutes later, their conversation over, she let out a shaky breath of relief before punching the air in excited triumph. Brad had not only endorsed her proposals for the campaign, he had actually also allocated a more than generous budget to cover the cost of running her ads on TV.

There was still an enormous amount of work to be done, of course, and Brad had stressed that the timing of the TV campaign was vitally important and that it must coincide with the completion of Kyle's revamping of the technical side of things.

'To offer a service we can't follow up on would be counter-productive, to say the least,' Brad had told her.

'Suicidal,' Star had agreed.

'Kyle's due to fly back to Britain tomorrow,' Brad had informed her. 'He'll fix up a meeting with you to go over everything we've discussed and I guess he'll have his own input to make. It will make sense to have any actors who feature in your ads as service engineers dressed in whatever uniform Kyle decides his contract people will wear...'

'Mmm...' Star had agreed with him. 'And, of course, so far as the visual impact of a TV campaign is concerned, the colour of the technicians' uniforms or whatever could be very important. It has been proved scientifically that different colours cause different emotional reactions in people.'

Whilst they had talked she had made notes of the

points that Brad had raised and now, as her initial euphoria subsided, she studied them.

This contract, this campaign, was the high spot of her career, a triumphant breakthrough, rewarding not just her persistence, her hard work and her single-minded concentration but also her gift for innovation and creativity—so why had Brad's confirmation that he fully endorsed her campaign left her feeling somehow empty and unsatisfied? Why was the once familiar thrill of succeeding somehow just not there?

Why, instead of feeling good about herself and what she had achieved, did she feel much the same as she had done as a child of ten years old when she had won an important scholarship, only to have her mother protest that it didn't do for girls to be too clever—boys didn't like it—and for her father to be too wrapped up in his new wife and family even to remember what she had achieved by the time he eventually got around to seeing her?

What was *wrong* with her? she asked herself hardly. She was an adult now, not a child. She had no need of anyone to praise and compliment her. She didn't need the approval and congratulations of others to make her feel good about herself... It was enough for her to know what she had done. She looked at the phone. Perhaps she could ring Lindsay and they could go out for dinner together, only no doubt Lindsay would be too busy now that she and Miles were reconciled.

What *was* the matter with her? she wondered irritably as she found her throat closing up on a lump of self-pitying emotion for the second time in twenty-four hours.

Perhaps she was suffering from some stress-related illness and that was what was making her feel so unfamiliarly weak and vulnerable. Yes, that was probably it, she decided quickly. What she needed was an early night and some decent sleep.

*   *   *

Star had just curled up in bed when the phone rang. Sleepily, she reached for the receiver, her whole body going into shock as she heard Kyle's voice.

'Star, are you OK?' she heard him ask intuitively as she drew in her breath and tried to clamp down on the tell-tale sensations swamping her. 'Have I rung at a bad time?'

'I was trying to get an early night,' she told him coolly, once she had got her breath back. 'What do you want…?'

'Do you mean you're in bed?' he asked her, ignoring the second part of her conversation.

'That is normally where I go when I want to sleep,' Star confirmed sardonically, and asked again, 'Why are you ringing, Kyle? What do you want?'

There was a brief pause and then Star nearly dropped the receiver when he told her huskily, 'If I told you you'd probably hang up on me…'

Kyle, flirting with *her*. Kyle, coming on to her. Star couldn't believe her ears.

The words 'try me' rose to her lips but she quenched them firmly and said crisply instead, 'Brad rang me earlier to confirm that he's happy with the campaign.'

In his office Kyle smiled ruefully to himself. Was Star backing off from a sexual challenge? Either he had made a lot more progress than he had dared hope—or a hell of a lot less.

'Yes. He's approved everything you want to do,' he said, without telling her how much time and effort he had put into persuading and convincing Brad that the expense of running a TV advertising campaign could be justified.

That was the main reason why he had stayed over longer than he had originally planned. It had taken all the will-power he possessed and more not to telephone Star before now, and right now just hearing her voice was enough to make his body ache so much that he had to grit his teeth against his need.

'Look, it's going to be late tomorrow when my flight gets in and I was wondering if you could possibly do a little grocery shopping for me?'

Star was tempted to refuse but instead she heard herself asking, 'What exactly is it you want me to get?'

'Oh, just the basics,' Kyle responded vaguely. 'You know—milk, bread, that kind of stuff. It's going to be going on for midnight before I get in. My sister gave me enough home baked stuff to dangerously overload my luggage before she left. Not that I'm complaining; it was good to have her staying; it gave us an opportunity to catch up on one another's news.'

Star expelled a ragged breath. It had been his *sister* who had been staying with him and not another woman, a potential lover!

'If you want to leave it in my flat, Amy has a key.'

He held his breath, hoping she would say that she'd wait up for him, and then released it when she made no response.

Star didn't make any response because she was wondering why he had seen fit to leave Amy a key and not *her*, and wondering as well why she should feel so uptight about it.

'Well, I guess I'd better go and let you get back to sleep,' she heard Kyle telling her. 'Congratulations, by the way. Brad was very impressed by your campaign, and with good reason,' he told her generously. 'I know you thought I was being deliberately obstructive over your original idea, but I'm behind you all the way on this one. You've got a very creative mind, Star, a very special talent, and I predict it won't be long before you're making the big agencies very edgy and nervous.'

Star gripped the telephone receiver tightly and stared at her bedroom wall.

Why? Why did it have to be *Kyle* who acknowledged

her success and paid tribute to her skills, and why on earth did she have to feel even more desolate and forlorn because he had?

Quietly and without saying another word she replaced the telephone receiver.

Kyle sighed as he followed suit. No doubt she had thought that he was being both patronising and sexist in congratulating her, but he hadn't meant it that way. *He* had no hang ups about a woman being professional and successful—in fact he applauded it.

Star frowned as she placed her bag of groceries on Kyle's worktop and opened his fridge door.

Inside were two cartons of long-life milk plus all of the other basic items she had assumed he wanted her to get.

Out of curiosity she checked the freezer, her mouth compressing as she saw loaves of bread.

Why had he made an expensive transatlantic call to ask her to shop for items he already had?

Perhaps he had forgotten he had them, she decided as she unpacked and put away her shopping.

The flat had been refurbished now but the plants in the kitchen and sitting room looked desperately thirsty.

Automatically she watered them, making soothing, clucking noises as she saw how rapidly they absorbed the moisture. Plants were, after all, living organisms that needed care and nurturing...just like human beings... She frowned again as her brain assimilated that thought. What was she trying to tell herself—that *she* needed care and nurturing...? Since when?

Quickly she finished what she was doing, but on her way out of the flat some impulse she couldn't resist took her not to the front door but to the bedroom. The bed was neatly made, with no sign, no imprint of Kyle's body on either the bed or his pillow, and yet she still went up to it, smoothing the fabric of the pillowcase with her fingertips, bending her head towards it and then picking it up.

She was still standing with it clasped in her arms when she heard the front door open. For a second she simply stood where she was, completely frozen, and then, in a panic, she dropped the pillow back onto the bed and hurried out into the hall to come face to face with Kyle.

'You're early,' she told him accusingly. 'You said you wouldn't be back until midnight...'

'I caught an earlier flight,' he told her cheerfully, looking over her head towards the open bedroom door.

'I...I was just checking to make sure everything was all right before I locked up,' Star told him quickly. 'I...I've put your shopping away.'

'Thank you.'

Uncertainly Star looked up at him, her mouth parting in a soft O of surprise as he bent his head and kissed her.

She heard the thud of his case as he dropped it and wrapped both his arms around her, and knew weakly that she really should protest, that such a lingering and almost lover-like kiss was scarcely necessary in acknowledgement of the simple, neighbourly task of getting his shopping. But instead she just stood where she was, letting the tender, persuasive warmth of his mouth dissolve the iciness which seemed to have lodged around her heart.

When Kyle finally removed his mouth from hers she opened her eyes and looked dizzily into his.

'I...I have to go,' she told him unsteadily.

'Yes,' he agreed gravely, reaching out and tucking an errant lock of her hair behind her ear. 'I think you do.'

Wordlessly Star watched as he opened the door for her and he waited whilst she walked across the landing to her own flat.

Once inside it, she closed the door and then leaned against it, closing her eyes and breathing deeply. How *could* a single, simple kiss affect her like that. She felt...she felt... She didn't want to acknowledge or examine *how* she felt, she admitted shakily. She was too afraid of what she might learn.

Once Star had gone, Kyle walked into his bedroom. The pillow she had been holding lay in the middle of the bed where she had dropped it. Smiling, he picked it up and restored it to its rightful position.

CHAPTER TEN

'RIGHT, everyone... Last one now, everyone smile.'

Star could feel the tension in her jaw as her mouth widened in obedience to the photographer's request. What with the video and the formal photographs as well as the various family members wanting to capture their memories of the ceremony on film, it was a wonder that there had been any time for the actual formalities of the marriage itself, she reflected ironically as the photographer signalled that he was finished with them and the assembled family group started to break up.

Kyle, who had been standing beside her, laughed as one after another of the triplets ran towards him, demanding to be picked up.

'He's certainly got a way with children,' her most recent stepmother commented tiredly as she watched her offspring clamouring for Kyle's attention. 'Of course,' she added, 'they do really miss the input they would get from a younger and more physically energetic father. Has Kyle any children?' she asked Star inquisitively.

'I have no idea,' Star returned shortly, before turning her back on her. She had already seen the assessing and unmistakably feline look of interest that Lucinda had given Kyle. Perhaps it wasn't just the triplets who were missing out on input from a younger and more physically energetic man, she reflected, watching Lucinda's unsubtle attempts to get Kyle's attention.

Oh, yes, Kyle was certainly a hit with her family, she admitted, even her father was impressed. Wearily she massaged her temples; the tension headache that she had woken up with this morning had gradually become more unbearable as the day progressed.

Kyle had suggested that they travel down to the wedding the day before and stay over an extra night, but Star had rejected that idea, claiming that she was too busy to take the extra time off work. Now, though, she was paying the price for her stubbornness with an aching head and a fraying temper.

It had shocked her to discover how much her father seemed to have aged and actually physically shrunk since she had last seen him. Standing next to Kyle, he seemed so much shorter than the younger man and yet her childhood memories of her father were of an impressively tall, powerful-looking man.

He still retained his vanity and egotism, though, Star had decided cynically when he had insisted on being photographed surrounded by his progeny and his wives, both past and present, only her own mother missing from the line-up. Star realised now that he had not asked after her mother, and made a point of going over to him to inform him that she was to marry Brian. His reaction was brusquely dismissive.

'He just doesn't care,' she fumed after he had walked away and she had gone back to Kyle, who had witnessed the exchange from a short distance away. 'He never cared about either of us.'

'You're wrong,' Kyle corrected her decisively. 'I'd say he's actually rather jealous...'

'Jealous? No way. He was the one who wanted the divorce.'

'Some men can never really let go. Their vanity demands that they are the controlling force in a relationship, the most loved. It strikes me that you and your mother had a lucky escape, Star,' he added wisely.

'A lucky escape? What on earth do you mean?' Star challenged him.

'Look around you,' Kyle instructed her, 'and tell me what you see...'

'My father,' she responded belligerently.

'Your father and who?' Kyle questioned patiently.

'My father and his children...the ones he really wanted,' she told him angrily. 'The children he really wanted and their mothers...'

'Mmm. Shall I tell you what I see?' Without waiting for her to answer he continued, 'I can see a man who cannot bear to be ignored, who must come first—a man who is quite happy to manipulate and undermine those he claims to love to ensure that he is always the prime focus of their attention. Look at the way he plays one person off against another, the same way he played you off against Emily—the same way, in all probability, that he played you off as a child against your mother and vice versa.'

Star immediately opened her mouth to deny what he had said, her eyes mirroring both her shock and her outrage.

He forestalled her. 'It's human nature for us to want our parents to be paragons and perfect, Star, especially when our contact with them is limited. I know, I've been there and suffered the consequences. It can be devastating for children when they realise that the mother or father they love so much isn't perfect—devastating enough to turn that love to deep-seated resentment and even hatred.'

Star spun on her heel and walked away from him, angrily reacting to his comments in much the same way as she might have done to someone physically probing a painful wound with a surgical instrument, but thereafter she couldn't help observing how accurate his assessment had been.

Her father *did* encourage his different families to compete for his attention, he *did* manipulate chaos rather than encourage harmony between them, sometimes even between different members of the same family group, and she was shocked to realise that, whereas in the past she had always thought of herself as the lone outsider to the charmed, extensive family unit that he had formed around himself, there were in fact several others who shared her painful isolation and exclusion from the family fold.

Withholding his love and his approval and singling out one particular person at a time for this treatment was something her father was adept at, Star recognised. And she had also recognised something else which was even more disturbing, she acknowledged as she watched the way that Kyle encouraged the smallest of the triplets, the one who had held back as the other two had yet again rushed into his arms, to come forward, deftly hoisting one child onto his shoulders, leaving both arms free to gather the remaining two.

The look of relieved, grateful joy that radiated from the third small face made Star bite down hard on her bottom lip. What she had finally realised was that Kyle would never behave like her father. He would never willingly or wilfully hurt anyone, much less someone he professed to love. Kyle was different…Kyle was—

'Thanks…for coming.'

The hesitation in Emily's voice as she came to join her made Star quell her normal hostile response to her stepsister.

'You look beautiful,' Star told her, and meant it. 'Dad looked so proud as he walked you down the aisle.'

'Did he?' Emily gave her a surprised complacent look. 'He wasn't at all pleased when I told him that David and I were going to get married. David's been married before, you see, and John made a big thing about him marrying me on the rebound. He knew David's first wife and, according to him, David was desperately in love with her. It brought it all back for me, of course—how

desperately jealous I was of you as a child and how
desperately jealous my mother was of yours.'

'*You* jealous of *me*?' Star stared at her. 'But *you* were
always his favourite... You were the one he—'

'No, I wasn't.' Emily cut her off, shaking her head
decisively. 'Oh, I know it may have seemed that way,
but he was always comparing me with you, saying how
much cleverer you were, how much prettier. Everything
I did you had done before me and so much better—even
though you were younger. Just as everything Mum did
your mother had done before her and so much better.'

She pulled a wry face. 'I didn't want any of this, you
know,' she told Star, gesturing towards the lavishly expensive marquee thronged with guests. 'I wanted to get
married very quietly...for it just to be me and
David...but John made such a fuss... He kept going on
about the huge wedding that David and Naomi had had
and what people were going to think and say if we didn't
do the same. He wanted me to have all the children as
attendants, you know—*all* of them,' she stressed mean-
ingfully, 'including you...'

'What?'

Emily laughed as she saw Star's look of revulsion.

'I told him you'd never agree—thank God. And of
course you know what he's like—he had to make a big
thing of it, claiming that I didn't want you because I'd
always been jealous of you and then insisting that if all
his children couldn't be included then none of them
should be. Not that I minded. I was more than happy
with David's two nieces as my bridesmaids.'

'I should think you were,' Star said feelingly, unable
to stop herself from mentally counting up all her father's
children and then looking at the triplets who were still
with Kyle.

'I know; it doesn't bear thinking about, does it?' Emily murmured, reading her mind.

'No, it doesn't,' Star agreed.

They looked at one another and then burst out laughing, the laughter in Emily's eyes suddenly turning to bright tears as she reached out and hugged her fiercely, saying emotionally, 'Oh, Star, I so much wanted you as my sister, but somehow we never got it quite right did we?'

'No...no, we didn't,' Star said grimly, and then to her own surprise she heard herself saying, 'But that doesn't mean that we still can't.'

'No, it doesn't, does it?' Emily agreed, giving her another fierce hug.

'Ready to go?' Kyle asked a few minutes later, deftly avoiding a would-be rugby tackle from someone's child as he crossed the hotel lawn to join Star.

Heavens, he was like a modern-day Pied Piper, Star decided in fascination; none of the children, it seemed, could keep away from him.

'What on earth is it about you?' she asked him distastefully. 'Your aftershave?'

'Nope.' Kyle laughed good-humouredly. 'Nothing special; I just like kids.'

'So I see,' Star responded disdainfully. 'Let's hope your wife, when you do marry, is equally enthusiastic; after all, she'll be the one who ends up playing the major role in their upbringing.'

'Not necessarily,' Kyle corrected her. 'I'm quite happy to be a house-husband father if things work out that way.'

Star digested his statement in silence as he drove them back to their hotel. Her tension headache had spread to her neck and the muscles of her shoulders and upper back now and she instinctively tried to ease the stiffness out of them.

Kyle frowned as he saw her discomfort and asked her in concern, 'Are you OK?'

'I've just got a bit of tension, that's all,' Star answered him brusquely. She wasn't used to anyone showing con-

cern about her health; her relationships with men had
never included that type of intimacy.

'Don't worry, I know just the thing for it,' Kyle assured her as he turned into the drive that led to their
hotel.

'So do I,' Star snapped.

Typically Kyle refused to take offence or retaliate,
simply smiling at her as he parked the car. Uncharacteristically, Star let him take the lead in dealing with the
receptionist.

The day had drained her both emotionally and physically—as she had guessed it would—but for very different reasons from those she had imagined.

She was amazed at how easily and how dispassion-
ately she had been able to watch her father ignore her
and turn to fuss with the triplets instead. And she had
felt for them, rather than experiencing her normal sense
of humiliation and shame at being passed over in favour
of her father's other children.

Their suite was large and comfortable, with two bedrooms and bathrooms and a shared sitting room. Star,
like Kyle, carried her own overnight case, and she was
just about to put it in her room when Kyle told her quietly, 'I've arranged for the bill to be made out to me;
we can split the cost later. I thought you'd prefer it that
way rather than have your father pay.'

She stopped and stared at him, unable to say a word,
her eyes filling with quick, irrational tears, and virtually
stammered a low, 'Y-yes...thank you...I would.'

How had he known that she would feel like that? she
marvelled as she walked into her room. That she would
want...? She put down her case and closed her eyes.
From the other side of the half closed door she heard
Kyle saying, 'I've ordered a room service meal—if
that's OK? I didn't think you'd want to bother going
down to the restaurant, but if—'

'No...no, that's fine,' she assured him wearily. Her head had started to ache really badly; all she wanted to do was to get undressed, have a warm, relaxing bath and then lie down.

She closed the bedroom door and started to remove her suit.

'Star?'

Groggily Star opened her eyes. She was lying on her front. Kyle was standing at the side of the bed, looking down frowningly at her. Her room was in semi-darkness and as she glanced automatically at her watch she realised that she had been asleep for over two hours.

'What happened to dinner?' she demanded huskily, wincing as she moved and discovered that the tension from her headache had remained in her neck and shoulders.

'I cancelled it,' Kyle told her drily. 'We can always reorder later. How do you feel?'

'Lousy,' she told him feelingly.

'Perhaps I can help; where does it hurt?'

'What are you doing?' Star demanded breathlessly as he placed his hand on the bare skin of her naked shoulders and gently started pressing the tense muscles.

'Giving you a massage,' Kyle responded easily. 'It's a proven fact that it's just about the best way to relieve stress-induced tension.'

'A massage!' Star started to sit up and then subsided as she remembered that she was completely naked.

'I don't need a massage,' she tried to protest crossly, but her body was telling a different story as it positively revelled in the sensation of Kyle's fingers easing the knots of tension from her taut muscles. Star tried to tell him to stop but her demand was muffled by the pillow as Kyle pressed more firmly into the knotted tissue.

'No wonder you've got an aching head,' he told her wryly. 'The whole of your back feels like it's virtually seized up. Breathe deeply and slowly,' he instructed her, 'and we'll do this properly; you feel like you need it.'

She felt like she needed what? Star wondered edgily. If it had been another man she would have been highly suspicious of that type of comment, but Kyle, of course, was different.

'There you go, tensing up again,' she heard Kyle complain as her body reacted to the message that her brain had just given her. Kyle was different. Kyle *was* different.

An odd sensation, a combination of breathlessness, light-headedness and exhilarated relief, burst upon her, causing her to feel somehow as though she had just laid down an extraordinarily heavy burden that she had been forced to carry. She opened her mouth to tell Kyle about it and then closed it again as her habitual protective caution reasserted itself. As she turned her head she saw a neat pile of clothes on the chair next to her own and recognised that they were Kyle's.

'Just stay right where you are,' she heard him instruct her before she could ask what he was doing. 'I'll be right back.

'Here you are; you can lie on this,' he announced several seconds later as he emerged from her bathroom carrying a huge bath towel. 'I haven't got any massage oil but I guess this will do...'

'Massage oil?'

Star's head whipped round. Kyle was standing beside the bed holding what looked like a courtesy bottle of some kind of body oil. He had stripped off to his underwear—a pair of snugly fitting black briefs.

The sight of a man in his underwear was not one that Star normally found in the least erotic. In her opinion men looked sexy either fully dressed or wearing nothing at all; a man wearing briefs and, even worse, his socks in her view looked totally unalluringly and ardour-dampeningly coy. But in Kyle's case...

She gulped and tried to look somewhere else. From the way her pulse was starting to race it was just as well that he hadn't stripped off completely, she thought.

'I don't think this is a good idea...' she started to say, but Kyle refused to listen.

'It's OK, I know what I'm doing,' he told her. 'I had a lot of practice when I was in my teens.'

'Thank you,' Star told him through gritted teeth, 'but I do not want to hear an account of your youthful sexual adventures...'

'My youthful sexual adventures? What have they got to do with this?' Kyle asked her. 'Like I was saying...I had a vacation job one summer, working for the coach of the local hockey team. He swore by a thorough massage for relieving heavy bruising and muscle strains... He was the one who taught me how to do it...

'It's a pity we don't have a proper table, but I suppose the bed will have to do,' he added, whipping away the duvet before Star could protest.

Unlike him, she *had* removed all her clothes, and for some reason she did not feel in the least mollified when Kyle tactfully draped a small towel over the rounded curves of her behind.

'Now try to breathe slowly and deeply and just relax,' he instructed her.

'Just relax'. And how on earth was she supposed to do that when he—? Star stiffened in startled surprise as she felt him start to knead not her shoulders as she had expected but her foot.

'It's my back that's stiff, not my feet,' she protested.

'Your whole body is stressed out and tense,' Kyle informed her firmly. 'Now keep still and just relax. A good massage should be a pleasurable, enjoyable experience...'

Star looked back over her shoulder suspiciously but Kyle's head was bent as he concentrated on massaging her calf and she couldn't see his expression—couldn't see *his* and quite definitely didn't want him to see *hers*, she acknowledged as she fought to suppress the very definite quiver of sensation that shot up her leg and which she knew perfectly well had nothing to do with the efficacy of a good massage and everything to do with the efficacy of the massager.

By the time he had reached the top of her thigh, Star was both gritting her teeth and curling her hands into two small, agonised fists beneath the controlling protection of the pillow.

'I don't understand it,' she heard Kyle protesting. 'It just doesn't seem to be working. You're every bit as tense as you were when I started...'

On the contrary, Star could have told him, it was working only too well, but in a rather different way from the one he had obviously envisaged.

'Well, there isn't much point in going on, then,' Star said in relief, but Kyle shook his head.

'No, my guess is that what you need is a whole course of treatment with a qualified physio...'

'You're probably right,' Star agreed. 'I'll organise something.'

'I'll just try and see if I can free some of the tension from your back,' Kyle told her, adding, 'You'll have to move further down the bed, though, so that I can come to that end and work that way...'

Work that way...? Work what way? He surely didn't mean...?

But apparently he did, and Star smothered a small, protesting groan as Kyle pushed the pillows out of the way and positioned himself on the bed in front of her. Did he *have* to kneel there like that? she wondered indignantly. And if he did...if he did... Dizzily she closed her eyes. Weren't men past the youth of their teens and twenties supposed to lose muscle tone and develop potbellies, especially those of them who were desk-bound executives?

Kyle didn't... Kyle hadn't...

'You really are in a bad way,' she heard him complain as he leaned over her and placed his hands on her back. 'You're actually twitching.'

Twitching... He would twitch if he... She smothered another groan as his fingers stroked slowly over her spine. She didn't know which was having the more destructive effect on her self-control—the sensation of him touching her or the sight and scent of him. The sight at least she could blot out, but the scent...his scent...

There was no masking the shudder that tormented her as Kyle worked his way over her back, and it was almost a relief when he found the flat, hard lump of knotted muscle which had formed as a direct result of her tension and worked on it, causing her to gasp with pain.

'It's all right,' he assured her soothingly.

All right? Oh, of course it was all right, Star decided helplessly. After all, all he was doing was reducing her to a helpless, gibbering wreck of agonised female desire—an aching, tormented, thoroughly aroused bundle of female cells and hormones.

As she ground her teeth against the moan of arousal that she could feel rising in her throat, Kyle asked solicitously, 'Did that hurt? Sorry...'

Star had had enough.

'No, it did not hurt,' she told him forcefully, wrenching herself out of his hands.

'Turn over, then,' Kyle suggested, 'and I'll—'

Turn over!

Star closed her eyes. 'I can't,' she told him in a small, mortified voice, and then added despairingly, 'Kyle, will you please put some clothes on?'

'On.' He was actually laughing wickedly at her, Star recognised as he released her. 'I kinda hoped you were going to ask me to take them off.'

'Off?' Star tried to sound quellingly acerbic but she

knew her voice was trembling and she knew her body
was as well.

'Yes, off,' Kyle said encouragingly as he gently but
firmly turned her over and bent his head to kiss her
gently, but not so gently that the effect didn't ricochet,
rampaging from one end of her body to the other, Star
noted in despair as she tried to resist what was happening
to her. But how could she resist when, instead of assist-
ing her, Kyle was just making the situation worse by
continuing to kiss her?

She tried to say as much but the movement of her lips
as she tried to form the words somehow or other gave
Kyle the idea that she actually wanted him to continue
kissing her and in the end it was simply easier to be
acquiescent—easier and oh, so very much more pleasurable.

Kyle was still stroking her skin but his touch was very
definitely a sensual and deliberately erotic caress now.

'Have you any idea what you've just been doing to
me, how much you've been turning me on?' he whispered into her mouth as he opened it with his tongue.

'Tell me about it,' Star moaned back feelingly, her
whole body shuddering with delight as his open palm
slid over her breast, the tip of his thumb rubbing tor-
mentingly against her nipple.

'Mmm…you taste so good,' she heard him telling her
appreciatively as he nuzzled his way down over her
throat and between her breasts.

'So good,' he repeated far more hoarsely as his tongue
circled her navel and her towel was removed.

Star had thought of herself as sexually sophisticated
but there was nothing sophisticated about the way she
was reacting now, she recognised—about the way her
whole body, but most especially her thighs, had started
to tremble, about the sensations and emotions that
gripped her as she felt Kyle's mouth open and move
down over her body.

Such intimacies…such emotions surely belonged to true lovers and should be exclusively *their* domain but there was no denying her need to respond to and reciprocate the intimacy of Kyle's lingering oral caress.

Helplessly, she reached out to him.

For a moment she thought that he either didn't truly comprehend or didn't want to respond to her own need but after a second's hesitation he removed his briefs and watched her, his expression unreadable as she moved her body and then bent her head towards him.

He felt hard, powerfully hard to the touch and yet at the same time very humanly vulnerable. He didn't move but Star was aware of his quick indrawn breath as she placed her lips against his thigh and slowly started caressing him.

She wasn't sure which of them shuddered more deeply when she finally touched him with her tongue, delicately rimming a circle around him, but she knew that her own reaction to the feel and taste of him was so intimately powerful and explosive that she could actually feel her body tightening in sensual urgency.

'Star!'

The hoarse sound of her name was enough to make her pause and look at him. His face was slightly flushed, a dark burn of colour highlighting his cheekbones and his eyes. Star trembled, as shaky as a newborn colt, when she saw the look in his eyes.

'I want you,' she told him helplessly, unable to stop herself from responding vocally to the look he had given her.

'Nowhere near as much as I want you,' he retorted fiercely. 'Nowhere near as much.'

She had always known instinctively that there would be strength and power in those arms, in that body—but what she had not guessed was that that strength would empower her and allow her, for the first time in her life, actually to enjoy her own vulnerability, to feel that it was safe for her to allow someone else to take control, to know that she could trust him...that she was safe with him...

She cried out to him when he eventually entered her, unaware of what she said, unaware of having told him that she loved him, unaware of anything other than the almost violent surge of pleasure that engulfed her as the tight circle of her need snapped.

Star had known physical pleasure before but she had never known this emotional completeness, never known such overwhelming joy in the aftermath of any previous intimacy, never wanted to hold and be held by any previous partner the way she did with Kyle.

But then she had never loved anyone as she did him, had she...? She had never loved anyone at all...until now... Until Kyle.

Star woke up in the middle of the night suddenly and sharply aware that Kyle was no longer there in bed with her. Her eyes searched for him in the darkness and found him, standing motionless in front of the window, his head bent, his expression sombre and almost brooding. In a flash Star guessed what was wrong, what must be on his mind. Her love for him overwhelmed her. Immediately, she got out of bed and padded over to him, touching him gently on the arm.

'Kyle...'

He looked silently down at her.

'I know what you're thinking,' she told him, 'but it...it isn't like you think... I wasn't... I didn't...'

She took a deep breath, her voice soft with emotion as she told him, 'You haven't really broken your vow...about not having sex with someone but only making love... Not really.' She paused; this was so very difficult for her. Her pride alone was enough of an obstacle to overcome, never mind the fact that she was stripping away her defences and allowing Kyle to see her so nakedly vulnerable. She could see that he was frowning.

'Star…' he began, but she placed her fingers over his lips and gave him a look that was both fiercely determined and touchingly appealing.

'No…please let me finish,' she begged. 'This isn't easy for me. It goes against everything I've always believed in, everything I've always said and done, but I can't let you think—' She stopped and swallowed and then said huskily, 'It just wouldn't be fair… It wasn't just sex,' she told him bravely. 'What we did…what we *shared*,' she emphasised, 'was…' She swallowed again, moistening her nervously dry lips. 'We *did* make love with emotion and involvement,' she told him, looking down at the floor, unable to look directly at him any longer. 'At least I—'

She stopped.

'You what?' Kyle challenged her sharply, his voice sounding slightly rusty—probably because he was feeling so bad about what had happened, Star decided sympathetically. It was still such a new emotion to her, this sense of feeling for someone else, of wanting—no, needing—to put him first, to put his happiness above her own.

'I made love,' she told him firmly, finally managing to lift her head and look squarely at him. 'I…I made love and I— Kyle, Kyle…what are you doing?' she protested as he suddenly swooped and picked her up in his arms.

'What am I doing?' he repeated, his eyes and his mouth warm with laughter and with something else as well, Star recognised as her heart suddenly started to bounce against her chest wall like a rubber ball on elastic. 'What I am doing,' he said, 'is taking you back to bed where I fully intend to keep you until I get a verbal repetition of that statement you just made and where I

intend, as well, to give you my own response to it, both
vocal and physical.

'Now tell me again,' he demanded as he lowered her
onto the bed and gently but firmly held her there.

'Tell you what?' Star queried, tongue-in-cheek.

'Tell me,' Kyle insisted between deliciously erotic
kisses, 'what you know damn well I want to hear.'

'That I made love?' Star repeated huskily, keeping her
gaze fixed on him. 'That we didn't just have sex? That
for me that—?'

'No,' Kyle corrected her softly. '*We* made love. This
time and every time,' he promised her. 'And the reason
we made love is because we *do* love... I love you and...'

'I love you,' Star whispered shakily to him. 'Kyle, I
love you,' she repeated, reaching out to shake his shoulder as she tried to communicate her own sense of wonder
and awe at what she had so recently discovered.

Kyle watched her indulgently before pulling her into
his arms and telling her provocatively, 'I know you do...
I knew it all along.'

'You...you what...?' Star tried to protest, but Kyle
took the expedient measure of silencing her by kissing
her and kissing her...and kissing her.

Star snuggled closer to him.

'Mmm...'

'Mmm...' Kyle agreed as he lowered her back against
the bed.

EPILOGUE

'AND to think that if I hadn't told you the night of Emily's wedding that it wasn't, at least on my part, just sex between us—because I hated to see you looking so...down, because I realised that my love for you was far, far stronger than my need to win and make you think that I'd triumphed because you'd broken your vow—none of this would have happened,' Star told her husband lovingly as she reached up and kissed him.

They had been married very quietly earlier in the day—a church ceremony with only their closest friends present. Sally, bloomingly pregnant and joyously happy, had escorted Star down the aisle in lieu of her father—Star's own decision. She had explained to her father that in view of their complicated family history and the fact that not all of Kyle's family could fly over for the ceremony they had decided against an ultra-traditional wedding.

Her mother had been there, with Brian, and so had Brad and Claire. Her father, characteristically, had sulked and announced that he would not be able to attend as a mere guest since he and the family were going away on holiday.

'Don't let it hurt you,' Kyle had told her gently when she had read her father's letter.

'It doesn't,' Star had responded simply and truthfully. 'He *is* still my father and always will be, but I see him differently now; I see him as he is and not as I want him to be, thanks to you. It doesn't hurt any more, Kyle,' she assured him. 'You have healed all my hurts.'

Emily and David had also been at the wedding. A friendship, a closeness that Star could never have envisaged existing even as short a time as twelve months ago had developed between her and her stepsister.

Sally and Star's friendship had strengthened and deepened too and Sally had already intimated that she wanted Star to be godmother to her soon-to-arrive baby.

'I can't promise to be a traditional wife and mother like Claire and Poppy,' Star had warned Kyle the night before the wedding. 'I can't change the person I am.'

'Star, I don't want you to change,' Kyle had told her firmly. 'I fell in love with you as you are. I *love* you as you are,' he had stressed.

Now, in the privacy of their honeymoon-suite bedroom, listening to her reflecting on that all-important night they had spent together, Kyle started to laugh.

'What are you laughing for?' Star demanded.

'I don't think I dare tell you. Not until after we've consummated our marriage; that way at least you'll have to wait to divorce me instead of merely getting an annulment...'

'*What* are you talking about?' Star asked warily. By now she knew all about his quirky sense of humour and how much he enjoyed teasing her.

'That night you're talking about,' he told her more seriously, 'I wasn't brooding about the possibility that I might have broken any promises to myself...'

'Yes, you were,' Star insisted. 'I could see it in your face. You looked so...so sad, so despondent and I knew what you must be thinking. I knew how important your insistence on not having sex without love was to you.'

'Yes, it was important,' Kyle agreed candidly. 'But never anywhere near as important as you. And besides,' he added softly, taking her in his arms, '*I* already knew that *we* had made love and not merely had sex...'

'What?' Star struggled to break free of him as she glared up at him. 'How could you possibly have known that? Even I—'

'You told me,' Kyle interrupted her gently. 'You told me when I was loving you how much you cared, how much you needed me...how much you loved me...'

'Did I?' Star looked uncertainly at him, inwardly digesting what she had just learnt. 'Oh,' she said, and then added, 'So there was no need for me to... I didn't have to... I could have...'

'There was no *need*,' Kyle agreed. 'But that doesn't mean that I didn't and don't appreciate what you did and said, my darling, nor that I don't realise how difficult it must have been for you to overcome all those inbuilt prejudices and fears.'

He bent his head and kissed her and then withdrew his mouth a breath away from hers as she struggled to speak.

'Well, if you weren't looking so unhappy about that, then what was bothering you?' she asked him curiously.

'You,' he came back promptly. 'You might have told me you loved me in the heat of the moment, so to speak, but I knew how much you'd hate revealing something which you would see as vulnerability and how much you'd resent me for being the cause of it. I didn't just want your loving...your *love* in bed physically...I wanted it wholly and completely and I wanted you to want me in the same way. If I looked despairing it was because I was wondering just how the hell I was going to achieve that kind of miracle, and then you solved the problem for me...'

Just before he bent his head to resume kissing her, his attention was caught by something on the small table next to them. He reached out and picked it up, holding it out to Star for her inspection as he whispered in her ear, 'It's the room-service menu. It's got sea-bass on it. Want some?'

'Hmm... I'm not so sure... Perhaps I should just have a taste of yours,' she responded provocatively.

They were both laughing as Kyle picked her up and carried her towards the bed.

The bouquet arrived with the room-service waiter and the sea-bass. Attached to it was a small card on which Sally had drawn a small cartoon character punching the air in triumph and written the words, 'Yes! Yes!! Yes!!!'

Laughing helplessly, Star showed it to Kyle.'Strange things, these old superstitions,' Kyle told her, his words muffled through their shared kiss. 'It doesn't do to treat them lightly or to mock them. You just never know what might happen.'

'No,' Star murmured back happily, 'but I think I know what's going to happen now!'

EVER HAD ONE OF THOSE DAYS?

TO DO:

☑ late for a super-important meeting, you discover the cat has eaten your panty hose

☑ while you work through lunch, the rest of the gang goes out and finds a one-hour, once-in-a-lifetime 90% off sale at the most exclusive store in town (Oh, and they also get to meet Brad Pitt who's filming a movie across the street.)

☑ you discover that your intimate phone call with your boyfriend was on company-wide intercom

☑ finally at the end of a long and exasperating day, you escape from it all with an entertaining, humorous and always romantic Love & Laughter book!

ENJOY
LOVE & LAUGHTER™
EVERY DAY!

For a preview, turn the page....

Here's a sneak peak at
Colleen Collins's RIGHT CHEST, WRONG NAME
Available August 1997...

"DARLING, YOU SOUND like a broken cappuccino machine," murmured Charlotte, her voice oozing disapproval.

Russell juggled the receiver while attempting to sit up in bed, but couldn't. If he *sounded* like a wreck over the phone, he could only imagine what he looked like.

"What mischief did you and your friends get into at your bachelor's party last night?" she continued.

She always had a way of saying "your friends" as though they were a pack of degenerate water buffalo. Professors deserved to be several notches higher up on the food chain, he thought. Which he would have said if his tongue wasn't swollen to twice its size.

"You didn't do anything...bad...did you, Russell?"

"Bad." His laugh came out like a bark.

"Bad as in *naughty*."

He heard her piqued tone but knew she'd never admit to such a base emotion as jealousy. Charlotte Maday, the woman he was to wed in a week, came from a family who bled blue. Exhibiting raw emotion was akin to burping in public.

After agreeing to be at her parents' pool party by

noon, he untangled himself from the bed sheets and stumbled to the bathroom.

"Pool party," he reminded himself. He'd put on his best front and accommodate Char's request. Make the family rounds, exchange a few pleasantries, play the role she liked best: the erudite, cultured English literature professor. After fulfilling his duties, he'd slink into some lawn chair, preferably one in the shade, and nurse his hangover.

He tossed back a few aspirin and splashed cold water on his face. Grappling for a towel, he squinted into the mirror.

Then he jerked upright and stared at his reflection, blinking back drops of water. "Good Lord. They stuck me in a wind tunnel."

His hair, usually neatly parted and combed, sprang from his head as though he'd been struck by lightning. "Can too many Wild Turkeys do that?" he asked himself as he stared with horror at his reflection.

Something caught his eye in the mirror. Russell's gaze dropped.

"What in the—"

Over his pectoral muscle was a small patch of white. A bandage. Gingerly, he pulled it off.

Underneath, on his skin, was not a wound but a small, neat drawing.

"A red heart?" His voice cracked on the word *heart*. Something—a word?—was scrawled across it.

"Good Lord," he croaked. "I got a tattoo. A heart tattoo with the name Liz on it."

Not Charlotte. Liz!

HARLEQUIN PRESENTS®

Three women make a pact to stay single...
But one by one they catch

and then the magic begins!

Don't miss this compelling new trilogy
from bestselling author

Take a trip to the altar in:

June 1997—BEST MAN TO WED? (#1889)
July 1997—TOO WISE TO WED? (#1895)

Available wherever Harlequin books are sold.

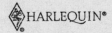

Let's Celebrate!

LOVE & LAUGHTER™

invites you to
the party of the season!

Grab your popcorn and be prepared to laugh
as we celebrate with **LOVE & LAUGHTER**.

Harlequin's newest series is going Hollywood!

Let us make you laugh with three months of terrific
books, authors and romance, plus a chance to win a
FREE 15-copy video collection of the best romantic
comedies ever made.

For more details look in the back pages of any
Love & Laughter title, from July to September,
at your favorite retail outlet.

Don't forget the popcorn!

Available wherever
Harlequin books are sold.

 HARLEQUIN®

Look us up on-line at: http://www.romance.net

LLCELEB

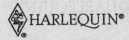

New York Times Bestselling Authors

JENNIFER BLAKE
JANET DAILEY
ELIZABETH GAGE

Three *New York Times* bestselling authors bring you three
very sensuous, contemporary love stories—all centered
around one magical night!

It is a warm, spring night and masquerading as legendary
lovers, the elite of New Orleans society have come to
celebrate the twenty-fifth anniversary of the Duchaise
masquerade ball. But amidst the beauty, music and revelry,
some of the world's most legendary lovers are in trouble....

Come midnight at this year's Duchaise ball, passion and
scandal will be...

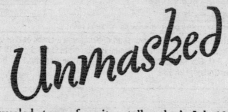

Unmasked

Revealed at your favorite retail outlet in July 1997.